She wanted to dist███

She found herself intrig███

He turned his head into the light, a gesture that allowed her to see his face for the first time without dark shadows hindering her inspection.

His sharp, serious eyes and tall, lean body reminded her of a big beautiful cat. Unwavering, patient. And very, very dangerous.

Code name: Cougar.

It fit him to perfection. With his dark blond hair, piercing blue eyes and strong, obstinate jaw he could hail from any number of northern European countries. Austria, Norway, Great Britain.

Germany.

She turned from *that* disturbing thought and focused her full attention on her understudy, pretending grave interest in the other woman's enthusiastic compliments.

Unable to stop herself, she slid another glance at her contact from beneath lowered lashes. The watchful look in his eyes suddenly vanished and, just as quickly, a pleasant smile rode across his lips.

The effortless charm put her on instant alert.

He shoved away from the wall and began pacing toward her. Slowly, deliberately. The hunter stalking his prey.

Books by Renee Ryan

Love Inspired Historical

*The Marshal Takes a Bride
*Hannah's Beau
Heartland Wedding
*Loving Bella
Dangerous Allies

*Charity House

Love Inspired

Homecoming Hero

RENEE RYAN

grew up in a small Florida beach town. To entertain
herself during countless hours of "lying out" she read
all the classics. It wasn't until the summer between her
sophomore and junior years at Florida State University
that she read her first romance novel. Hooked from
page one, she spent hours consuming one book after
another while working on the best (and last!) tan of
her life.

Two years later, armed with a degree in economics
and religion, she explored various career opportunities,
including stints at a Florida theme park, a modeling
agency and a cosmetics conglomerate. She moved on
to teach high school economics, American government
and Latin while coaching award-winning cheerlead-
ing teams. Several years later, with an eclectic cast of
characters swimming around in her head, she began
seriously pursuing a writing career.

She lives an action-packed life in Lincoln, Nebraska,
with her supportive husband, lovely teenage daughter
and two ornery cats who hate each other.

RENEE RYAN
Dangerous Allies

Steeple
Hill®

Published by Steeple Hill Books™

STEEPLE HILL BOOKS

Steeple
Hill®

ISBN-13: 978-0-373-82844-9

DANGEROUS ALLIES

www.SteepleHill.com

Printed in U.S.A.

I am sending you out like sheep among wolves.
Therefore be as shrewd as snakes
and as innocent as doves.
—*Matthew* 10:16

To my dear friend and BBS co-founder, Staci Bell. Thank you for your support through the years. You might buy all my books, but I'm your biggest fan!

Chapter One

20 November 1939
Schnebel Theater, Hamburg, Germany
2200 Hours

They came to watch her die.

Every night, they came. To gawk. To gasp. To shake their heads in awe. And Katarina Kerensky made sure they never left disappointed.

Tonight, she performed one of her favorites, Shakespeare's *Romeo and Juliet*. In typical Nazi arrogance, Germanizing the arts hadn't stopped at simply eliminating "dangerous" persons from cultural life. The Chamber of Culture had continued its purification function by also ruling that Shakespeare—in German translation, of course—was to be viewed as a German classic, and thus acceptable for performance throughout the Fatherland.

Leave it to the Nazis to claim the English playwright as their own.

In spite of her personal reasons for hating the Third

Reich, Katia loved the challenge of taking a role already performed by the best and making Juliet her own.

For a few hours on stage her world made sense.

Now, poised in her moment of mock death, her hair spilled past her shoulders and down along the sides of the raised platform on which she lay. She held perfectly still as her Romeo drank the pretend poison and collapsed beside her.

She could smell the brandy and sweat on Hans as the foul scents mingled with the mold growing on the costume he hadn't washed in weeks, but Katia thought nothing of it. She was a professional and approached the role of Juliet as she would any role, on or off the stage. With daring conviction.

Hitting his cue, George, the bald actor playing Friar Laurence, made his entrance. As the scene continued to unfold around her Katia remained frozen, her thoughts turned to the actors who should also be sharing the stage. She was one of the lucky ones. Instead of playing a star-crossed lover doomed for eternity, she could have been among many of her peers thrown out of the theater due to whispers—often untrue—of their Jewish heritage or socially deviant behavior.

For now, at least, she was safe. As she was the daughter of a Russian prince, Vladimir Kerensky, fame had been her companion long before she'd stepped onto a stage.

Would notoriety be enough to keep her safe?

The Nazi Germany racial policy grew increasingly violent and aggressive with each new law. If anyone checked Katia's heritage too closely they might discover her well-kept secret.

To the Germans, she was merely a real-life princess playing at make-believe. A natural, as her mentor Madame Levine had always said. Good skin. Innate talent. Beautiful face and hair. All added to the final package. But the brains? Katia kept those hidden behind the facade of ambition and a seemingly ruthless pursuit of fame.

If the Germans only knew how she really used her talents. And why.

Opening her eyes to tiny slits, she tilted her face just enough to cast a covert glance over the audience. Her latest British contact was out there waiting. Watching. Bringing with him another chance for her to fight the monster regime and protect her mother with means she'd been unable to use to defend her father.

She drew in a short breath and focused on becoming Juliet once more. The scent of stage dust and grease-paint was nearly overpowering. Dizzying. The spotlight blinding, even with her eyelids half-closed. Nevertheless, Katia remained motionless until her cue.

"The lady stirs...."

As though in a trance, Katia rose slowly to a sitting position. She fluttered her eyelashes and let her arms drag behind her. Arching her back, she held her arms limp, making the motion appear effortless.

Presentation, Madame Levine had taught, was the difference between a rank amateur and a true artist.

Pitching her voice to a hoarse whisper, she said, "O, comfortable friar! Where is my lord?" The muscles in her arms protested, but she continued to hold them slack.

Katia wrapped her temporary role of the doomed Juliet around her like a protective cloak then tossed a confused, sleepy look over the audience. "I do remember well where I should be." She sent the audience a long, miserable sigh, then wiped the back of her wrist across her brow. "And there I am."

Pushing a shaky smile along her lips, she let it cling to the edges of her mouth for only a moment before hiding it behind a pout. "Where is my Romeo?"

Friar Laurence tugged at her as he began his impassioned speech to make her leave the tomb with him.

Ignoring his pleas, Katia peered around. She blinked once. Twice. Then turned her head away from the audience.

Friar Laurence came to the end of his speech. "I dare no longer stay."

Katia focused her attention on the actor lying next to her, narrowing her performance down to this final moment. Nothing existed before. Nothing after. Just this handful of lines. A few moments when escape was possible.

Feigning horror at the sight of her dead husband, she allowed a lone tear to trail down her left cheek. In a tragic whisper she recited her next lines, pretended to search desperately for a drop of poison in the vial she rescued from Romeo's clenched fist, then listened to the lines spoken offstage.

She pulled her brows into deep concentration. "Yea, noise? Then I'll be brief." She made a grand show of searching Romeo's belt. On a gasp, she widened her eyes. "O happy dagger!"

Snatching the fake blade, she raised it high above her. Arching, she tossed back her head, snapped it forward again, then locked her gaze on to the thin blade. "This is thy sheath…"

With a dramatic flourish, she stabbed herself just above her stomach. "There…rust, and let me die."

Swaying, she sucked in her breath, buckled over in pain, and collapsed on top of Romeo.

As the rest of the cast trooped in for the final scene, Katia remained unmoving, only half listening to the words of the rest of the play.

Knowing her performance had been one of her best, she tried to ride the wave of success. But the joy remained elusive this evening, as it had each night since the Nazis had discovered Madame Levine's fraudulent papers.

And just as the Lord had done back in Russia during the revolution, God had abandoned Germany. Now most of the people Katia loved were dead, imprisoned or worse.

Her mind raced back to the last time she'd seen her mentor, now shipped off to Neuengamme, for her lie as much as for her Jewish heritage. There had been no warning, no time to help.

Would Katia's mother be next? The quick burst of fear came fast and hard at the thought.

Why didn't Elena Kerensky see that no one was safe in Nazi Germany, not even Russian royalty? Why didn't she understand that the very people who had killed Katia's beloved father—for no reason other than his distant relation to the Romanovs—were no different than the Nazis? Hitler could easily broaden his definition of a Jew to include anyone with only one Jewish grandparent, rather than the current definition of two.

At that thought, fear played in Katia's head, taunting her and convicting her. She would not allow her mother to die for so small a reason.

Katia was no longer a helpless eight-year-old witnessing the death of her loving father and loss of her beloved homeland. She was no longer an innocent who believed prayer was the answer, that God cared enough to stop the violence. As an adult she put her trust only in herself, not in a hard-hearted God who allowed courageous men like Vladimir Kerensky to die at the hands of their enemies.

At least now, as a British informant, she had the means to protect one of her parents.

A sense of control surged. The power of it danced a chill up her spine, giving her a foundation of order beneath the chaos.

The actor playing the Prince of Verona said his final line, dragging Katia back to her immediate job for the evening. "For never was a story of more woe than this of Juliet and her Romeo."

The applause broke out like a rumbling stroke of thunder. With a convicted heart, Katia rose to take her bows.

She was ready to begin her next mission, ready to fight the Nazis, ready to stop the tyranny before it swallowed up her mother and others like her.

* * *

Avoiding the crush of people milling around backstage, Lieutenant Jack Anderson leaned a shoulder against the wall behind him and watched Katarina Kerensky in action. She accepted the congratulations from her fellow cast members and adoring fans with understated grace.

In stark contrast, the overbright laughter and din of heavily accented voices sounded like a gaggle of geese, rather than a celebration of a remarkable woman's acting triumph.

Out of instinct and years of training, Jack surveyed his surroundings. He eyed the tangle of ropes and pulleys on his right, the large circuit box on his left. Extra props were set in every available spot. Dusty costumes lay strewn over a large paint-chipped box. There seemed to be no order, no organization. A full hour in this world and he knew the chaos would drive him mad.

The putrid odor of sawdust, human sweat and unwashed costumes took away the mystique of the fantasy world he'd watched come alive less than an hour before. From his seat in the twelfth row, the actors had glittered under the lights. Here they looked haggard, wilted.

Except for one.

The woman he'd come to meet was a surprise. And he was only half-sorry for it. Even as the thought rolled around in his mind he realized he should have had some instinct, some internal warning, that this mission wasn't going to be as tidy as the new chief of MI6 had claimed. Not with a woman like Katarina Kerensky involved.

Clearly, the British had a hidden agenda. But were they using this mission to ferret out individual loyalties, or was there a darker motive? Had the spymasters grown to distrust Jack and set a trap for him? Or was Kerensky their target? Given Jack's direct relationship with Churchill, the latter was far more likely.

Jack now admitted, if only to himself, that he hadn't prepared enough for his first glimpse of the famous actress. His sudden inability to catch an easy breath was like having a destroyer deposited on his chest. Later, when he was alone, he would sort through his messy emotions and decide what to do with them. For now, he had to disconnect. Focus.

Analyze the potential dangers.

She turned in his direction, tilted her head slightly and fixed him with a bold stare. Their gazes locked and held. A jolt of discomfort shot to the soles of his feet. He fought to keep his breathing slow and steady. But this woman made him *feel*.

The emotion wasn't real. It couldn't possibly be real.

And yet…

The sudden flash of vulnerability in her eyes before she buried the emotion behind a bored expression gave her an air of innocence that Jack didn't dare consider too closely. It was simply a well-honed weapon in her female arsenal. He had to remember she was an actress *and* a spy. Nothing but lies would come from her mouth.

With a mental shake, he pushed aside his initial reaction to the woman and focused only on measuring her as a potential ally. Or enemy.

He quickly took in the hair, the face, the perfect fit of her costume. Her skin was smooth and flawless. Her features delicate. Her eyes were large and slightly slanted, the color of the sea in a bitter storm. Her hair was a deep auburn, almost chocolate except when the light hit it and revealed an array of gold, red and orange.

Absently, Jack shoved at his own hair, surprised to find he was sweating. Blinking, he shook himself from the trance she'd put him in.

She was good. He'd give her that. But with those fabulous eyes no longer locked with his, the unsteady rolling in his gut slowed. She may have knocked his brains around—which was probably intentional—but Jack was back in control of his wits.

Before tonight he had always believed the Bible's David a fool to let a woman turn him into a murderer and adulterer. But Jack hadn't fully understood the power of a beautiful woman.

Or the danger. Until now.

Chapter Two

In spite of the dim lighting backstage, Katia easily picked out her contact by the single bloodred rose he wore on his lapel. He stood on the fringe of the post-production party, his face hidden by the shadows. She couldn't decide if the lack of light made him appear mysterious. Or sinister.

He lifted two fingers in silent salute then settled his broad shoulder against the wall behind him once more.

Katia didn't particularly like the way he watched her with those long, speculative looks. The quiet intensity in him made her heart beat in hard jerks. How much did he know about her? Did he know her secret?

A sense of unease skittered up her spine, but she boldly kept her eyes on his. She drew a careful breath. The man made her nervous. The tingling weakness in her limbs distressed her further, until she realized he was deliberately trying to intimidate her.

Another man who underestimated her.

Annoyance replaced her anxiety. Katia hiked her chin

up a notch. Many before him had seen her as a liability. And, like them, this one would ultimately come to view her as his greatest asset.

Or he would fail.

As he continued to study her with those smart, patient eyes, she felt a quick churn of hope in her stomach. But that made no sense. She refused to allow his assessment to go unmatched. With equal intensity she ran her gaze across him.

On the surface he looked like a young, wealthy German out for an entertaining evening at the theater. Dressed in an expensive tuxedo, black tie and crisp white shirt, he could pass as a financier. Maybe a bored aristocrat. Even one of Hitler's secret agents or a henchman for Heinrich Himmler.

Her breath came short and fast at that last thought. Did the Nazis know she was a mole for the British? Had they sent this man to trap her?

If it wasn't for the red rose, she'd give in to her fears. The operative's behavior certainly wasn't helping matters. His stance was anything but friendly. The intense control he held over his body spoke of hard physical training. Probably military. An officer, no doubt. A man used to giving orders, and having them obeyed.

She wanted to distrust him immediately.

She found herself intrigued instead.

He turned his head into the light, a gesture that allowed her to see his face for the first time without dark shadows hindering her inspection.

His sharp eyes and tall, lean body reminded her

of a big cat. Unwavering, patient. And very, very dangerous.

Code name, Cougar.

It fit him to perfection. With his dark blond hair, piercing blue eyes and strong, obstinate jaw he could hail from any number of northern European countries. Austria, Norway, Great Britain.

Germany.

She turned from that disturbing thought and focused her full attention on her understudy, pretending grave interest in the other woman's enthusiastic compliments.

Unable to stop herself, she slid another glance at her contact from beneath lowered lashes. The watchful look in his eyes suddenly vanished and, just as quickly, a pleasant smile rode across his lips.

The effortless charm put her on instant alert.

He shoved away from the wall and began pacing toward her. Slowly, deliberately.

The hunter stalking his prey.

A little stab of panic penetrated her attempts at calm. No. She would not show weakness.

He stopped in front of her, an inch closer than was polite, then offered a formal nod. Her understudy melted away, muttering something about needing a plate of food.

The scent of musk, expensive tobacco and dominant male was far too unsettling, the handsome face far too attractive.

In a purely self-defensive move, Katia gave her head an arrogant little toss. Lifting a single eyebrow, she concentrated on the planned greeting she was supposed to use with him tonight. "Did you enjoy the play?"

He nodded and stuck to the script, as well. "It was enlightening."

The words rolled off his tongue in perfect German, with just a hint of Austria clinging to the edges.

Relief had her fear smoothly vanishing. He was her British contact, after all.

She kept to the words MI6 had given them for this first meeting. "I'm glad."

"Perhaps we could discuss the finer points of your performance in a more private place?"

She swallowed but held his stare. He was following the script, so why did she get the sense he was toying with her? "Yes, I would like that."

His smile deepened in response, revealing a row of straight, white teeth. Her heart gave one powerful kick against her ribs. The charm was there, urging her into complacency, and yet his eyes were so stark and empty.

For a moment she glimpsed something that looked like despair behind his flawless performance, giving her the impression that this man needed someone to reach him, perhaps even to save him.

For a second she felt herself softening toward him, but only for a second. This was no romantic interlude. This was a serious game of war. Loss of control, even for a moment, meant death. And then who would protect her mother?

Katia quickly adjusted her thoughts by focusing on

her mother and all they had to lose if Katia became reckless.

She started to take a step back but her contact captured her hand, turned it over and studied her palm.

Her pulse raced at his light touch.

Not wanting to draw attention to them, she tried to ease her hand free, but he released her first.

"Perhaps we should go to…" He allowed his words to trail off, as planned, giving her the choice of the location for their real meeting.

Happy to take the lead, she cocked her head toward a room off to her right. "My dressing room is just over there."

Her territory.

His smile turned into a roguish grin. "Perfect."

The boyish tilt of his lips made her want to believe everything he said from this point on, even when she knew—knew for a *fact*—he made his life telling lies and using intrigue to accomplish his mission.

She opened her mouth to speak, reconsidered and then snapped it shut. Let him take command for a while, as expected.

"You were remarkable," he drawled, his words no longer following their scripted first meeting. His expression dared her to remark on his audacity.

She couldn't. She was too busy trying to shove aside the pleasure that swelled inside her at his impulsive remark. If there was anything she didn't trust it was a spontaneous, sincere compliment. It hit at a vulnerable spot deep within, the place no one had touched since her father's murder. The place that had once believed in a loving God.

She lifted a shoulder, pretending his deliberate shift in the conversation didn't bother her in the least. "Dying onstage has its own unique drama. Poetic and sizzling." She smiled, opened her heart just a little. "Wonderful, really."

His eyebrows drew together in an expression of genuine fascination. "Is that why you do it, then? For the drama?"

They both knew he wasn't talking about the stage.

Oh, he was a smooth one, intentionally forcing her further off track with an intriguing question. She would not be defeated by such a transparent maneuver. "Among other reasons."

She slanted him a warning glare. His questions were getting too personal. Too insightful. Too…dangerous.

Just how much did this man know about her?

Their association was supposed to be simple. But the curling in her stomach told her this mission had become entirely too complicated already. She had to remember they would work together only three days, then never see each other again.

She wouldn't even learn his real name. As far as she was concerned, he was Friedrich Reiter, a wealthy shipbuilder who frequented the theater.

Pushing the spark of remorse aside, Katia touched his arm, but then quickly dropped her hand at the shocking sense of comfort she felt on contact. "Why don't we—"

Her words were drowned out by voices coming from the backstage door leading into the alley.

Happy greetings rang out, one after another. Katia turned toward the sound of a familiar feminine voice, barely catching sight of her elegant mother before being greeted with a kiss on her cheek.

Taking a step back, Katia scooped a breath into her lungs and tried to focus her chaotic thoughts.

What was her mother doing here, tonight of all nights? Elena Kerensky rarely attended the theater and she never appeared backstage. Mingling with the masses was simply *not* done. It was one of her mother's cardinal rules.

So what had sparked this unprecedented visit?

Katia took another long breath and swept a furtive glance over her mother. Elena Kerensky was still a striking woman at forty-seven, one who knew how to dress for any occasion. Tonight, she'd chosen a form-fitting gown of ice-blue that matched the color of her eyes. She'd pulled her pale blond hair into a refined chignon, showing off the expensive jewels around her neck. The ensemble made her look every bit the brave Russian princess in exile.

"My darling Katarina." Elena spoke in her trademark breathy whisper. "You were lovely this evening. Perfectly charming. I am a very proud mother."

For a moment Katia's practiced facade deserted her. She, unlike her mother, had very few rules in life and only one unbreakable commandment: never, under any circumstance, involve her mother in a mission.

She had to send Elena on her way before propriety

required Katia to introduce the MI6 operative. Even though he had backed off a few steps, most likely to give her room to deal with this unexpected interruption, he remained close.

To further complicate matters, her mother wasn't alone. She'd brought her favorite escort of late, Hermann Schmidt, a cold-hearted naval officer in his early fifties.

Despite the air clogging in her throat, Katia needed to concentrate. What was Elena thinking? Not only did Schmidt hold the high-ranking position of captain in the *Kriegsmarine,* he had an unholy obsession for the Fatherland and a stark hatred of Jews.

Perhaps her mother didn't recognize the risks. Or perhaps she was simply hiding in plain sight.

"Katia, my dear, you remember Hermann?" Elena swept her hand in a graceful arc between them. "It was his idea to come backstage and congratulate you personally."

Which could mean…anything.

Far more worried about her mother's safety than the British operative standing to her right, frightening possibilities raced through Katia's mind, each more terrible than the last. Her heartbeat slowed to a painful thump… thump…thump.

How could her own mother willingly choose to align her loyalties with a Nazi like Hermann Schmidt? It was true, the Nazis hated the Communists as much as Elena Kerensky did, but that did not make them—or this man—her ally. Especially when Elena carried such a dangerous secret hidden in her lineage.

Katia would have to speak to her mother in private. But not now. Now, she had to don the comfortable role of silly, spoiled daughter. "Good evening, Herr...*Korvettenkapitän*. It is always a pleasure to see you."

Schmidt's eyes narrowed into hard, uncompromising slits. "It is *Kapitän zur See*, Fräulein Kerensky. Just as it was the last time you made the same mistake. And the time before that."

"Oh, dear, of course."

Arrogant beast.

Tossing her head back, Katia gave a little self-conscious giggle. "My apologies. I never seem to be able to distinguish the ranks of the *Kriegsmarine*."

She continued chattering nonsensical words that indicated her ignorance of all things military, ever mindful of the British operative moving back to her side once again. Beneath her lashes, she slid a covert glance his way, quickly catching the doubt in his bearing.

And why wouldn't he be suspicious of her now?

Katia's mission was to help him gain access to the blueprints of a Nazi secret weapon, a revolutionary mine that had sunk countless merchant ships over the last three months. Yet here she was, fraternizing with a U-boat captain.

Then again...

Perhaps she could use the Nazi's unexpected appearance to her advantage. How was the British spy to know that Hermann Schmidt was not one of her most useful contacts?

The key was to keep Hermann thinking she was an imbecile, all the while convincing the British operative she was a brilliant actress in a necessary performance to protect her mother.

Tricky. But achievable.

Elena, however, provided the one complication Katia could not defuse with any of her well-practiced roles. "Darling, please do us the honor of introducing your... *friend.*"

Chapter Three

The moment all three gazes turned toward Jack his gut twisted into a hard knot. For a fraction of a second all the intense emotions—the guilt, the anger, the need for vengeance—threatened to break free and sweep away his control. But if he relaxed his guard for a moment, no matter the cause, someone would end up dead tonight.

Hardening his resolve, Jack searched Kerensky's face for signs of a hidden agenda. There was obvious distress in her eyes, a clear indication this interruption was not planned. But the woman was a world-renowned actress, one who knew how to drag sympathy out of a man.

He would be a fool to trust her.

As though sensing his reservation, she flashed him a smile and he lost his train of thought. Clenching his jaw, he forced his heartbeat to settle. Yet, no matter how hard he concentrated, he couldn't look away from those remarkable eyes staring into his.

Kerensky blinked once, twice, finally breaking the spell between them. "Herr Reiter," she began, addressing him by his assumed alias. "This is my mother, Elena Kerensky, and her escort, Hermann Schmidt."

Acknowledging the woman first, Jack took Elena's hand and touched his lips to her knuckles. "It is an honor to meet you. I now see where Katarina gets her beauty."

"Thank you, Herr Reiter. You are very kind." She turned to her companion and motioned him forward. "Come, Hermann, say hello to Katarina's friend."

As expected of all loyal Germans, Jack stepped back and gave the required Third Reich salute. "*Heil* Hitler, *Kapitän zur See*."

The Nazi returned the gesture with quiet relish. "*Heil* Hitler."

On the surface, Hermann Schmidt looked like a typical naval officer, but there was something in his arrogant stance that turned Jack's blood to ice—an unyielding ruthlessness that he'd seen in too many high-ranking Nazis.

It was the same look that now stared back at him from the mirror every morning.

Was Jack becoming one of them?

Was he losing the last shreds of his humanity?

With each new mission, he played roulette with his soul. He could no longer expect God to hear his prayers or his pleas. Not after the horrors he'd committed in the name of war.

There could be no turning back, no chance of forgiveness. He had to start thinking like the man he was: a man with no future, no hope and a single goal—to hunt and destroy the enemy that had stolen his life from him.

Patience, Jack told himself. In spite of the urgency of his current mission, in spite of the tight deadline, time was his ally. He'd worked too hard building his cover to let an unexpected player in the game throw him off balance now.

Cutting through his thoughts, Elena Kerensky cleared her throat. "Herr Reiter, I don't believe we've met before. Have you known my Katia long?"

Jack noted the concern in the woman's eyes and decided to use it to ferret out how far Kerensky was willing to go to help the British.

"I've known *Katarina*—" he rolled her name off his tongue in a slow caress "—long enough to come to the conclusion that she is a remarkable woman whom I wish to know better."

Hitting her cue perfectly, Kerensky slid her arm through his and smiled up at him with unmistakable affection. "What a lovely thing to say, darling."

With surprisingly little effort, he returned her smile as though they'd already become lovers.

Her gaze filled with female vulnerability, and she snuggled closer to him.

He ran a fingertip along her cheek.

There was a time when the God-fearing man Jack had once been would have been appalled by their blatant sexual undertones. But that was before Jack had walked with the enemy, before he'd become an embittered U.S. sailor infiltrating the SS.

Much like this famous actress, he played whatever role was necessary to accomplish his mission.

And yet…

As he stared into Kerensky's beautiful green eyes, Jack couldn't stop himself from wishing they'd met at another time, and under different circumstances. He wondered if her performance was a remarkable display of acting ability, or something else. Something inherently truthful? Or something coldly sinister?

In that instant, the words of his father came to him. *Always remember, Jack, a woman has more power to destroy a man than any other weapon.*

Jack's pulse soared through his veins. Was Kerensky playing both sides? Had the Germans found out about his deception? Were they using this accomplished actress to bring him down at last?

Subterfuge. Hidden agendas. Jack no longer knew where the intrigue ended and reality began. Even in his own mind he could no longer discern how much of Jack Anderson lived inside him, and how much had become Friedrich Reiter, the deadly SS henchman. Every new mission blurred the line between the two, threatening Jack's soul bit by bit.

A smart military man always knew when to hold his ground, and when to retreat. For now, his work was done.

Tapping into the ruthless man the Nazis had created, the one who coldly witnessed brutalities without flinching, Jack extracted himself from Kerensky's grip. Ignoring the sense of loss that took hold of him, he turned to her mother then nodded at Hermann Schmidt. "It was a pleasure meeting you both."

Keeping his eyes on Kerensky's face, he took her

hand in his and raised it to his lips. "I look forward to our next meeting, my darling."

She made a soft sound of distress, but they both knew she wouldn't voice an argument in front of her mother and the Nazi officer. It was a small victory, to be sure, but a victory that put Jack firmly in control of the mission.

He couldn't have planned a more perfect finale to their first meeting.

Katia stared in muted astonishment as the British spy turned on his heel and headed toward the exit with ground-eating strides.

What now?

A wave of nausea hit, and for the first time all evening her smile threatened to waver. She stood perfectly still until the moment passed.

The man had gunmetal nerve, she'd give him that. Not only had he antagonized a high-ranking Nazi and her own mother with his boldness, he'd left Katia to deal with the messy consequences. Yet, even with frustration burning at the back of her throat, something about the British operative left her wanting…what?

What was it about the man that urged her to let down her guard, if only for a fraction of a second? For a moment tonight, with their arms twined together and their gazes bound in intimate familiarity, she'd forgotten all about playing a role. She'd merely been a woman enthralled with an intriguing man.

From the first moment their gazes had locked and held, she'd sensed her British contact was someone who knew what it meant to be an outsider. Just like her.

Was he a man she could trust?

A lethal thought.

Blind faith, she reminded herself, was nothing more than weakness, a trap that ultimately led to a one-way invitation to the concentration camps.

Another sick spasm clutched in her stomach, but she held her expression free of emotion. If the operative said he looked forward to their next meeting, then she had to believe there would indeed *be* a next meeting.

All was not lost.

For the moment, she simply needed to concentrate on placating a stunned parent and her suspicious escort.

Sliding a quick glance toward her mother, Katia cut off a sigh of frustration. Elena stood tall, her full attention focused on the British spy as he left through the back door.

"I don't trust that man," she muttered, regarding the exit with suspicious eyes. "Tell me again how you know Herr Reiter?"

Rule number one in espionage was to keep as close to the truth as possible. "He is a dear friend, one I see whenever he comes to Hamburg on business."

Hermann Schmidt made a noise deep in his throat that sounded like a growl. "What, precisely, *is* his business?"

The uncharacteristic display of interest in her affairs chilled Katia down to the bone. This grim-faced Nazi was not a person with whom her mother should be spending her time. He was a formidable enemy, one who could ruin Elena if he uncovered her secret.

On full alert, Katia played her role cautiously. The key was to keep it simple. Consistent.

"I'm sure he told me once." She tapped a finger against her chin. "I seem to remember him saying he owned a company that supplies the Third Reich with materials for the war."

Schmidt's features turned hard and inflexible, matching the severity of his tightly buttoned uniform and crisp white shirt underneath. "What sort of materials, exactly?"

Katia blinked at his impatience, the cold heat of the dangerous emotion flashing in his eyes. Fortunately, to Hermann Schmidt, beautiful equaled stupid.

The knowledge gave Katia a surge of courage, and a strong conviction to play this role to her utmost ability. Fluttering her lashes, she placed her hand on his arm and gave him an empty smile. Now, if only she wouldn't throw up and ruin her act. "Is it really so important?"

"Yes." He leaned over her, his eyes communicating an unmistakable ruthlessness. "It is *very* important you try to remember exactly what sort of business Herr Reiter owns."

"You don't have to take that tone with me." Katia dropped her hand and pretended to pout, all the while gauging Schmidt's mood from below her lashes. Why would a mere naval officer care what a man like Friedrich Reiter did for a living?

Before Schmidt responded, Elena pushed in front of him and softened her expression. "Try concentrating, dear."

"Yes, all right, Mother. I shall try."

She let out a sigh, careful not to overplay her role. This was no game. One misstep and her mother's life could be in danger.

In truth, the British had told Katia very little about her contact. Standard operating procedure. For all she knew, Friedrich Reiter was exactly who he pretended to be—a wealthy Austrian shipbuilder.

Having stalled long enough, she drew her eyebrows into a frown. "Yes, I remember now. He is in construction. Or…shipbuilding, perhaps? One of the two."

Schmidt's lips flattened into a hard line. "Which is it? Construction or shipbuilding?"

She flung her hair over her shoulder, fully into her role in spite of the German's open hostility. "Who can remember such tedious details?"

"You seem to have no problem remembering countless pages of dialogue."

She gave him a pitying look and put the royal princess in her voice. "Herr Reiter is a patron of the arts and he adores me. Nothing else matters beyond that."

Although he quirked an eyebrow at her, Hermann Schmidt visibly relaxed. "Of course, how could I have forgotten where your priorities lie?"

The sarcastic twist of his lips gave Katia pause. Like so many of his kind, this man was far too sharp to fool for long.

It was time to change the subject.

"Let's not talk about Herr Reiter anymore." She turned her focus back to her mother. "I had no idea you were coming to the theater this evening. You said nothing of it this afternoon at tea."

A slow smile spread across Elena's face. She looked at her escort with a question in her eyes. "Should I tell her?"

He nodded slowly, but there was a possessiveness in his gaze that had Katia swallowing hard.

Elena took both of Katia's hands in hers and sighed. "Hermann and I have marvelous news to share with you."

Katia looked from one to the other. At the happy expression they exchanged, a sick feeling of dread tangled in her stomach.

Oh, no. Please, please, no. "What...what news?"

"We are engaged to be married."

"Why, that's..." Katia's breath caught in her throat. Even if the Lord had long since abandoned Katia, God could not be so cruel. "I...I'm speechless."

"I've been waiting for your mother for many years." Masculine pride danced in Schmidt's eyes as he spoke. And something more. Something dark and ugly. And very, very determined. "Now I have her at last."

Elena moved to the Nazi's side and positioned herself shoulder to shoulder with him. "As you know, Hermann and I were childhood friends, before I met your father."

"I remember." Katia had to sink her teeth into her bottom lip to keep from shouting at her mother to wake from the nightmare that held her in its clutches.

How could Elena, a devout Christian with a secret Jewish grandfather, agree to marry a man whose only god was Germany and whose professed savior was Adolf Hitler?

"Congratulations." She nearly choked on the words. "I am very happy for you both."

"Oh, darling." Elena pulled her into a tight embrace. "I am so glad you're pleased."

"I only want you to be happy," she whispered into her mother's hair before stepping back.

"Hermann has three days before he ships out again." Elena's breath caught in her throat and tears shimmered in her eyes. "It is my fondest wish that all three of us spend time together during his visit."

Three days? How was Katia to complete her mission for the British with her mother demanding all her time? An unprecedented flush of desperation made her words rush out of her mouth. "But I am in the middle of a play. I have to be here every night and I—"

"Don't worry, darling." Elena patted her hand. "We'll simply spend the days together then have a late supper after your performances." Her tone was full of determination, a tone Katia knew well. In this, Elena would not relent.

Katia's composure threatened to crack, then she remembered her British contact's open declaration for her affections.

The man's game had been an act, but a brilliant, impromptu one that could be used to her advantage now.

Her best chance was to continue the ruse. "I'm sorry, mother. I have already promised Herr Reiter I would spend the rest of the week with him."

Elena dismissed the argument with a quick slash

of her hand. "Cancel your plans. You must take this opportunity to get to know Hermann."

Knowing better than to argue at this point, Katia nodded. "Let me see what I can do."

Unused to having her wishes denied, Elena took the vague promise as complete agreement. "Good. Now that that's settled, we would like you to join us for a celebratory supper this evening."

Supper? Tonight?

Katia couldn't bear the idea of breaking bread with Hermann Schmidt. In truth, she feared it with all her heart. But she feared her mother being alone with the man far more. "I would like nothing better. Just give me a moment to change out of my costume."

Without looking back, Katia fled to her dressing room. Weary from the drama of the evening, she sat staring straight ahead and rubbed her left hand as if it ached. A shocking wave of panic gripped her heart, making her breath sit heavy in her chest.

Overwhelmed, she buried her face inside her palms and fought back the tears burning behind her eyelids.

She was so…incredibly…tired.

How she wanted to accept MI6's invitation to escape this godforsaken country and live in England for the duration of the war. But Katia couldn't leave Germany without her mother. And Elena Kerensky would never leave. Not with her recent engagement to her childhood friend, a man who happened to be a ruthless Nazi naval officer.

How would Katia protect her mother now?

Chapter Four

After bidding Elena and her escort good night, Katia shut the door with a soft click. Pressing her eyes closed a moment, she released a sigh of frustration.

The night had gone worse than expected.

Already, she could see that *Kapitän zur See* Schmidt was going to be a problem. It had been foolish of her to hope otherwise.

The female in her wanted to kick something in frustration. The royal princess in her had been trained too well to give in to the childish display of emotion. The spy in her needed to quit stalling and formulate a plan.

Glancing at the mail laying on the entryway floor, she decided to ignore responsibility a little while longer. Food first, plan second. She hadn't been able to touch her meal at the restaurant, not with Schmidt firing off pointed questions between scowls.

Clearly, the Nazi neither liked nor trusted her.

Good. At least she knew where she stood with the man. That would make her planning less complicated.

She would use her fiercest weapons of cunning, lies and schemes.

Oh, but she was in a despicable business. Thankfully, she'd created many roles for use in her arsenal. By taking on other personas she kept the real Katia separate from the spy.

Rounding the corner, she caught sight of a man lounging in a chair in her east living room. Her chest rose and fell in a sudden spasm, the only outward sign of her inner distress. Otherwise, she stared at the British operative with nothing more than mild curiosity on her face.

He'd tugged his tie loose and had left the ends hanging on each side of his neck. He'd also opened the top three buttons of his shirt, revealing a smooth expanse of corded throat muscles.

Even in his relaxed position, there was a hard edge to him that somehow complemented her feminine decor. This man was one hundred percent rugged male, the quintessential alpha. Although he sat in a chair covered with pink and yellow fabric, he radiated masculinity.

Which did nothing to improve her mood.

How many surprises must she endure in one evening?

"You have exactly sixty seconds to tell me what you're doing in my home, Herr Reiter." The calm, detached voice was one of her most useful tools.

For an instant she thought she saw a deep male appreciation in his eyes, but he blinked and the moment was gone.

She lifted her chin a fraction higher. "Well?"

He didn't respond. Nor did he rise to greet her, as

would have been the polite thing to do. Perhaps by remaining seated he was reminding her whom he considered in charge of the mission.

Unfortunately for him, he had the particulars wrong.

"You now have twenty seconds to start talking before I throw you out of my home."

Leaning farther back in the chair, he hooked an ankle across his knee then glanced at the clock on the mantel. "Actually, we're now down to fifteen."

Her earlier desire to kick something turned into an overwhelming urge to kick *someone*. By sheer force of will she reminded herself that this stranger was to be her partner for the next few days. Their success would bring the British closer to defeating Hitler. A heady prospect.

Katia might be able to carry out her end of the mission alone, but she needed Friedrich Reiter to deliver the plans to MI6. That did not mean, however, she had to make this conversation easy for him. "Tell me, Herr Reiter, how did you know where to find me?"

"It's my business to know certain, shall we say..." He made a vague gesture with his hand. "Things about you."

There was something in the way he met her gaze that brought matters to a very basic level between them. Another time she might have enjoyed the challenge of discovering the real man beneath the layer of polish and subterfuge. For now, she could only wonder what motivated him to risk his life for Great Britain. Personal gain, as most of the spies she'd met before him? Or was he answering a higher call?

Either way, the clock was ticking. She couldn't afford the luxury of delving into his inner psyche right now.

"What sort of...*things?*" she asked from behind a well-positioned smile.

He slowly unfolded his large frame and rose. As he strode toward her, she shrank back a step, as much startled by her reaction to him as by the intensity in his gaze. He stopped a mere foot away from her, his heat chasing away the sudden cold that had slipped under her coat.

For one small moment, time seemed to stop and wait for him to speak.

"For instance. Your mother never joins you backstage after a performance." His gaze stayed locked with hers. *"Never."*

Her fingers flexed by her side. Already, the man knew too much. "This evening was a rare but happy occasion."

"Special enough for her to choose a high-ranking *Kriegsmarine* officer as her escort?"

Katia stiffened. She should have known he would go straight for the heart of the matter. "Hermann Schmidt is a friend of my mother's. He is nothing to me." She nearly spat the last of her words. But not quite.

Eyes still locked with hers, Reiter moved yet another step closer then brushed aside a strand of hair that had fallen over her eye.

Katia held perfectly still.

"Did you know that your left eyebrow twitches when you're upset?" He tucked the hair behind her ear.

It took everything she had not to jerk beneath the impact of his soft touch. He was using familiar tricks against her, but she knew this role well. She'd worn it like a protective shield when she'd accepted the company of some of the vilest men in Germany in order to gather valuable information for the British.

The fact that Friedrich Reiter's blatant attempt to throw her off balance was working shifted the power in his favor. "Hermann Schmidt will not be a threat to our mission. I give you my word."

She was not surprised when he closed his hand around her arm. She was surprised, however, that his grip was gentle. In contrast, a rough warning filled his gaze before he released her.

He'd made his point.

"I trust no one's word, Katarina." No longer playing the role of seducer, his cold-eyed regard slid over her. "And I take nothing on faith. I believe only in my well honed ability to see through a lie."

With the steel in his voice and the military glare in his eyes, she almost buckled. *Almost.*

This man was formidable.

In spite of the pounding of her heart and the bead of sweat that slid between her shoulder blades, she had to stay focused. It helped to remember that without her, there was no mission.

"Well tonight, Herr Reiter, you are misreading the signs."

The air grew tight and heavy between them. His gaze

turned harsher, deadlier, the layers of polish peeling away to reveal a cold, merciless man.

But was the transformation real or just another act? Either way, she recognized the strategy of a back-alley brawler when she saw it. If this spy expected to intimidate her with his act, he was in for a disappointment.

Jerking her chin, she swept out of his reach and began roaming through the room. Step by step, she discarded her gloves, her coat and finally her hat.

On her second pass, she strolled within inches of him, proving to them both she was back in control of her nerves.

Obviously unaware of her internal struggle, he dropped into the wingback chair closest to him and flicked on a nearby lamp. Relaxing, he watched her in a very masculine way that sent her pulse skipping fast and hard through her veins. He played this game well.

"You seem to be making yourself comfortable," she said.

He gave her a crooked grin. The gesture transformed his features, making him look almost upright. Trustworthy. Decent?

Games inside games. Secrets inside secrets. How she hated the intrigue of espionage.

A jolt of weariness struck her then, making her feel hollow with an unfortunate mixture of exhaustion and doubt. She was not overly fond of the sensation.

"You might as well sit," he said, indicating the chair facing him. "This could take a while."

Knowing he was right, that the sooner they discussed

their mission the better, she cleared her expression and sank into the offered seat.

Before she could settle in, his demeanor turned all business. "Tell me how you know Schmidt?"

Katia gripped the arms of the chair until her knuckles turned white from the tension. She was growing more than a little irritated by the spy's lack of faith in her. *She* was the one with far too much to lose, while he would be free of this tyrannical country in a matter of days. "Hermann Schmidt is a friend of my mother's. End of story."

"How close are they?" he asked. *Asked.* Not demanded. Oh, no, nothing so crude. Had he demanded an answer from her, she would have known how to respond. But now, she was…confused. This cunning spy had his own repertoire of schemes and tricks.

With another sigh, she folded her hands in her lap and settled into their polite clash of wills. She decided to answer with the truth. "They are to be married shortly."

"When did they become engaged?" Although his expression never changed, his voice dropped to a low, hypnotizing timbre.

Nearly seduced by the soothing tone, dangerously so, Katia barely managed to keep from gritting her teeth. She wasn't used to handling a man this clever with his words, or this cunning with his voice. "I don't see the point—"

"When?"

She could feel the anger in him now. This interrogation had moved to a more hostile place.

Very well.

Katia knew exactly what to do with male anger. "I don't know, precisely." She spread just the hint of a pout across her lips. "They only told me the happy news this evening."

Happy news? Rage flowed through her at the ridiculous notion. The Russian Revolution had already stolen her father. And now the evil Nazi regime had its claws in her mother.

Memories of her dead father swept across her mind, coming stronger than usual tonight. No matter how illogical, she couldn't stop torturing herself over her failure in Russia.

She'd been too small, too insignificant to challenge the revolutionists. She had prayed, though. Without ceasing. For one full year.

God had remained silent.

By the age of nine, Katia had stopped praying altogether. She hadn't spoken to her Heavenly Father since.

With the hollowness returning to her stomach, Katia curled her hand into a tight fist. Never again would she count on an absent God who remained silent at her most desperate hours. Katarina Kerensky would do whatever it took to ensure her mother was spared the same fate as her father.

"You're upset by your mother's choice of husbands."

The unexpected softness in Reiter's voice had Katia shaking her head to keep her mind focused. She could handle his suspicion and distrust. She could even handle his subtle attempts at seduction—those were all part of the game they played—but this...this...*understanding?* It unnerved her.

"My thoughts on the matter are of no consequence." She spoke in a detached, unemotional tone. "The choice is hers to make."

"Nevertheless, you would have chosen differently for her."

There was that hideous compassion again. Open, honest and very real. Another game? A trap? "We are through with this topic. My mother has nothing to do with our current mission."

He opened his mouth to speak then shut it again and nodded. "Perhaps you're right. However, Hermann Schmidt—"

"Is my problem."

The spy's expression changed with the speed of a torpedo bearing down on its target. No longer relaxed, eyes hard, he sat coiled like a snake ready to strike. "Let's talk straight, shall we?"

"And here I thought we were."

Ignoring the interruption, he rose and moved to tower over her. "I've been given the task of stopping a Nazi naval secret weapon. Now pay close attention, Katarina. Imagine my shock when I meet my German contact at the assigned time, and a high-ranking officer in the *Kriegsmarine* shows up, as well."

"Mere coincidence, nothing more."

A dangerous glint flashed in his eyes. Katia tried not to squirm under his scrutiny. She wanted to stand, to move away from his ugly suspicion, but he blocked the path by crouching down in front of her.

"Coincidence?" He contained his energy well, but she knew he could strike at any moment. "There is no such thing."

She would not show fear. She would not draw away. She would go on the offensive instead. "Aren't you over-reacting just a bit?"

"I call it being cautious." He leaned forward, stealing nearly all of the space between them. "Will your mother's fiancé interfere with our mission?"

She knew he was crowding her on purpose, trying to intimidate her with his superior size.

The game was all about power now. *This* was a game she knew how to play, and how to win. "Choose whatever you wish to believe. I admit I am unhappy about my mother's impending marriage, but you must trust that I will handle Hermann Schmidt directly."

With a snort of disgust, he pushed away from her and returned to the chair he'd occupied a few moments earlier.

She started to explain, to clarify the situation for them both, but he cut her off with a hand in the air. "Is he one of your informants?"

It was an understandable question, one he had every right to ask. One she would answer truthfully.

"No." She held the pause for effect, gaining control from his surprised expression. "Hermann is simply my mother's fiancé, a man who hates the Communists as much as she does."

Reiter slowly sat back and steepled his fingers. "I see."

Unfortunately, Katia was afraid this man saw far too much. Would he prove more of a problem than Hermann Schmidt? Katia could barely contain a wave of terror at the thought.

But no matter how afraid she was, she would not give in to any outward sign of vulnerability.

Not until she was alone.

Blinking away her emotions, she lifted her chin. "Finish with your questions, Herr Reiter. You're fortunate. I find I am in an obliging mood, after all."

A single eyebrow lifted. "How do you plan to 'handle' your mother and her fiancé?"

In an attempt to gather her thoughts, she looked at the open window on her left. A light breeze joined in a ghostly waltz with the sheer curtains. The scent of coming snow shivered in the air, promising a thin coat of white by morning.

"I'll know more when I meet them tomorrow morning." Some unnamed emotion rose up. She shoved it back with a hard swallow. "They are picking me up at 0900."

"That's going to be a problem."

"Not if—"

"I go the rest of the way alone." The lethal expression in Reiter's eyes was enough to make even the bravest woman quiver in fear. She held his stare anyway, knowing that he was waiting to see what impact his declaration would have. She waited to see how long he would wait for her.

Games inside games.

The deceit and smoky undercurrents were growing with every tick of the clock.

Another minute passed.

And then another.

At last, Reiter broke the silence. "Tell me where the blueprints are hidden and I'll be out of your life forever."

"That won't be possible. You need me with you."

"You won't be available. You have a future stepfather to entertain." His voice was very soft. Very dangerous.

"You don't understand," she insisted. "You *need* me."

His eyes narrowed. "Why you?"

She didn't move, didn't breathe, afraid if she did she would break down and blurt out too much information. Keeping her secret to herself kept her and her mother alive. "Since I'm the one with the intelligence, you have no other choice than to rely on me."

His eyebrows slammed together. "In other words, if I don't allow you to come along, you won't tell me where the plans are hidden."

"That about sums it up."

"Are you trying to blackmail me, Kerensky?"

"Yes." But he didn't need to know why.

"An honest answer at last," he said, an odd hint of approval in his gaze.

His reaction threw her off balance. *Again.* What was she supposed to do with him now?

"Go ahead." He gestured for her to continue speaking. "You might as well tell me the rest, the part you're intentionally hiding from me."

She pretended to misunderstand him. "I don't know what you mean."

He simply looked at her.

She held perfectly still, dreading the obvious question to come. *Was she a Jew?*

But he surprised her once again.

"Tell me, Katarina," he drawled. "Why don't the British trust you?"

Chapter Five

Three. Four.

Five.

Jack counted each emotion that flashed in Kerensky's eyes. Up to this point, she'd proven herself inventive, bold and cunning, all necessary qualities for a spy. But in the soft moonlight, with so many emotions running across her face, she looked fragile, and surprisingly vulnerable.

In spite of Jack's distrust, a cold chill of fear for her took hold. If she *were* working for the British, which all the signs indicated, then she was playing a dangerous game with her life.

Why take the risk?

Jack had personally witnessed the hideous forms of torture the SS used to get answers. He'd watched in steely silence as the toughest men were utterly destroyed under the perfect blend of physical pressure and mental interrogation. The experience had cost him his soul. A reality he'd long since accepted, or at least lived with as atonement for his sins.

But now, as weariness kicked in, he didn't know if he could watch this woman suffer the Nazis' ruthless brand of interrogation. Unless, of course, she was working against him. Even then…he wasn't so sure.

The woman confused him. She made him want to return to simpler times, when the love of a sovereign God was concrete in his mind. When Jack had dealt with situations beyond his control by tapping into the knowledge that the Lord was bigger than any circumstance man could create.

But that was a long time ago, a lifetime ago.

Jack knew better than to take anything for granted, especially the actions of a trained professional.

Still on his guard, he gave Kerensky a look a few degrees short of friendly and continued waiting her out.

One beat, two beats, three.

At last, she broke. "The British don't," she began as she sucked in a harsh breath, "they don't trust me?"

Her reaction pleased him. The bitter resentment in her tone meant he'd actually shocked her. He had the upper hand now. Though he doubted she would accept the shift in power for long.

In his years as a spy, he'd never met a woman who could hold her own against him. Before Kerensky. Her determination was as forceful as his. For that alone, his gut told him to take a chance and trust her to do her share in the mission.

He restrained himself.

Until he discovered if she was an ally or a shrewd double agent he would not relax his guard.

"Look, Kerensky." He pushed to his feet. "Let's rid ourselves of this ridiculous power struggle and get on with the business at hand."

In response to his frankness, her composure slipped just a bit, but not enough to give Jack a sense of her real motives.

She was good. Very, very good.

With practiced grace, she stood and then paced through the small, stylishly furnished room. "If what you say is true and the British don't trust me, then it must be because they know about my…my mistake."

Her voice hitched. Part of her act? Probably. "What sort of mistake?" he asked.

Before responding, she roamed through a set of double doors with a liquid elegance that spoke of her stage training. Jack followed her, taking special note of how she gained immediate confidence once she had the physical barrier of an antique wooden table between them.

"It's not what you think," she said.

He willed himself to remain calm. In his line of work, losing his temper got a man killed faster than bullets. "It never is."

"You don't have to be snide. The information I gave MI6 was correct." She dropped her gaze to the table, drew a path of circles with her fingernail. "At least, it was at the time I sent it."

"Of course."

She slapped her palms on the table and leaned forward. "Your attitude is not helping matters."

"Nor is your penchant for withholding valuable pieces of information."

Head held high, she marched around the table and stopped long enough to let out a soft sniff of disapproval before she continued past him.

Keeping the woman in his sight, Jack trailed after her as she went back into the adjoining room and turned to face him. Folding his arms across his chest, he leaned against the doorjamb.

Neither said a word, each silently assessing the other. Jack considered the tactical scenarios and possible outcomes. The only wrong questions were the ones he didn't ask. "My patience is wearing thin. What mistake did you make, Katarina?"

Regardless of the flicker of uncertainty in her eyes, she held his gaze. Brave woman.

"Karl Doenitz moved his headquarters this morning."

Jack dragged a hand through his hair and resisted the urge to let loose the string of obscenities that came to mind. "How very inconvenient for us all. Except, of course, for the Nazis."

"Now you're being paranoid."

"I was trained to be paranoid." He drilled her with a hard glare. "And I'm very good at my job."

She sighed. "I realize this sounds bad, but Karl Doenitz is still in Wilhelmshaven. He's moved from Marinestation to Sengwarden."

Jack caught the quick, guilty glance from under her lowered lashes. "Which means you don't know where the plans are any longer."

"I—"

"This trip to Hamburg has been a waste," he said,

more to himself than her. "For nothing more than count-less hours of...*games*."

"Oh, I promise you, this is no game. I know where the plans are. It's just—" She broke off and looked away from him.

"It's...just?" he prompted with what he considered heroic patience.

Apparently, he could control the work, the decisions, even the risks. He could not, however, control this... *woman*.

"The plans are locked in a newly built cabinet. My key will only open the old one."

"That's it?" Jack had to resist the urge to laugh in relief. "That was your mistake?"

He'd dealt with worse. Much worse. Missions were always more complicated than they first appeared on paper. Real life had intricacies that tended to create a powder keg of unexpected problems.

"Are you just going to stand there staring at me?" she demanded. "Didn't you hear what I said?"

"I heard. You gave the British outdated infor-mation."

"I gave them *wrong* information. I never get it wrong. Never."

"Until now."

She inclined her head slightly, her expression giving nothing away. "Until now."

"So we make a new plan."

He didn't add that this was just the sort of tangle that had first led him into the heart of Germany two years before—the type of unexpected twist that ruled his every move. Disorder was so much a part of who he'd become, he'd long since accepted the realities of living without certainty. He didn't especially like the ambiguity of never knowing the outcome of a mission or when the next twist would come, but he bore the pressure with steely grit.

He had no other choice.

"Make a new plan," she repeated. "It's that simple for you?"

"Nothing is ever simple."

In fact, the possibilities were endless, but Jack was exceptionally skilled at finding the perfect solution inside the less perfect ones. "Tell me exactly where the plans are and I'll come up with an idea. Or better yet, get me some paper and something to write with. I think better with a pen in my hand."

She sank into a chair with an uncharacteristic lack of grace. "There is one more complication you should know about."

Jack felt like he was free-falling without a parachute. His tight control over dangerous emotions was slipping, and that made him furious. Nothing shook him, and no one caught him by surprise. Even when the real Friedrich Reiter had come to kill him, Jack had kept his wits about him enough to prevail in the deadly clash. There'd been no time for prayer, no begging the Lord for assistance, just reflex.

And now…here…with this woman…he was in another situation where his control was being tested.

Enough. The feminine manipulation ended now.

"Let's have it," he said, pure reflex guiding his words. "*All* of it."

"As you wish." Narrowing those glorious eyes of hers, she jumped up and planted a hand on her hip. "The admiral keeps the key to the cabinet on a ring he carries with him at all times, except when he sleeps. Whereby, he sets the key chain on the nightstand by his bed."

The roll in Jack's gut came fast and slick, surprising him. He didn't take the time to analyze the emotion behind the sensation. "And you know this how?"

Taking three steps toward him, Kerensky pursed her lips and patted his cheek. "That's my business, darling."

He grabbed her wrist. "Not if it's going to endanger my life."

"Which it won't." She dropped a withering glare to his hand, waited until he released her. "Now, back to what I was saying. Since I alone know where the key is located, all I have to do is sneak into the room while Doenitz is asleep and—"

"No." Whoever went in that building had to respond instantly if discovered. Jack was the trained killer. She was simply a mole who gathered information. He was the obvious person for the job. "*I* will break into the admiral's private quarters."

Her smile turned ruthless, deadly. The change in her put him instantly at ease. They were finally playing on his level.

He smiled back at her, his grin just as ruthless, just as deadly as hers.

She appeared unfazed.

"Here's the situation, Herr Reiter, and do try to pay close attention. There are only two ways into Admiral Doenitz's quarters. Through the front door or through a small window into his bedroom."

The thrill of finding a solution had Jack rubbing his hands together. "Now we're getting somewhere."

"The window leading into the admiral's room is small." She dropped her gaze down to his shoes and back up again. "Far too small for you."

"Then I'll go through the front door."

She was shaking her head before he finished speaking. "To get through the front door you would have to pass through six separate stations, with two guards each. They rotate from post to post on twenty-minute intervals, none of which are synchronized. Translation, that's a minimum of six men you would have to bypass at any given time."

"It's what I do."

She flicked a speck of dust off her shoulder. "Needlessly risky. Especially when I can get through the window and back out again in less time than a single rotation."

Jack's mind filed through ideas, discarded most, kept a few, recalculated.

"I'll ultimately have to get past those guards the night I go in for the plans," he said.

More thoughts shifted. New ideas crystallized, further calculations were made.

"I'll just take the key and the plans all at once." He blessed her with a look of censure, testing her with his words as much as with his attitude. "Translation: we go to Wilhelmshaven tonight and finish the job in one stroke."

She jabbed her finger at his chest. "You're thinking too much like a man. Go in, blow things up, deal with the risks tomorrow."

"Not even close." If anything, Jack overworked his solutions before acting on them. It was the one shred of humanity he had left.

"Two nights from now Karl Doenitz will be in Hamburg, at a party given for him by my mother." She raised her hand to keep him from interrupting. "And before you say it, that also means the key will be with him in Hamburg, as well."

"Keep talking while you get the paper I asked for."

She remained exactly where she was. *Naturally.*

"Here's how it's going to work," she said. "I get an impression of the key tonight, make a copy tomorrow, then go back the evening of the party and photograph the plans."

"Why not just steal the plans tonight and be done with it?"

"And alert the Nazis that the British have discovered their secret weapon? No." She shook her head. "We need to photograph the plans when no one is around and replace them exactly as we found them."

Her plan had a simplicity to it that just might work.

"And while I'm inside Doenitz's private quarters," she continued, "you get to do what men do best."

"And that is?"

"Protect my back."

If Jack didn't let his ego take over, he could see that

her idea had possibilities. Perhaps, under all the layers of subterfuge, they thought alike. Maybe too much alike.

The woman was proving smart enough and brave enough that if he let down a little of his guard he might begin to admire her. Too risky. Emotional attachments, of any kind, were a spy's greatest threat. Especially when he had no real reason to trust his partner.

"Your plan has merit," he said. "But I only have two more days to get the plans and return to England. With the timeline you presented, there's no room for mistakes."

She nodded. "Then we make no mistakes."

"We? Haven't you forgotten something?"

Her brows drew together. "No, I'm pretty sure I've thought through all the details."

"Your mother is throwing the party for the admiral. Your attendance at such an illustrious occasion will be expected. How are you going to pull off the last of our two trips to Wilhelmshaven while at a cocktail party in Hamburg?"

Her expression closed. "I'll handle my mother. She won't even miss me."

"And her fiancé? Somehow, I doubt he'll be so... inattentive."

"I'll deal with him, as well."

He gave her a doubtful glare.

"You're going to have to trust me."

Trust. It always came back to trust. But Jack had lost that particular quality, along with his faith in God, the same night the real Reiter had come for his blood.

"And if you're caught tonight?" he asked in a deceptively calm voice.

"I won't be."

"*If* you are."

She lifted her chin, looking every bit a woman with royal blood running through her veins. "Failure is never an option."

Jack's sentiments exactly.

If he took out the personal elements running thick between them and ignored the fact that Kerensky was a woman—a woman he couldn't completely trust—not only could her plan work, but it had a very high probability of success.

Her voice broke through his thoughts. "It's getting late. The drive to Wilhelmshaven will take almost two hours each way."

He glanced at his watch, looked at her evening gown and jewels then down at his own tuxedo. "We both need to change."

"Yes. We'll take my car, which is still at the theater." Which they both knew was only three blocks from her home.

"Right, then. We'll meet outside the theater at—" he began before he checked his watch again "—0130 hours. I trust that suits you?"

Head high, she moved to the front door and jerked it open without looking back at him. "Of course."

He reached around her and swung the door shut with a bang.

She spun about to glare at him. "What are you doing?"

Reminding us both who's in control.

With nothing showing on his face, he angled his forearm against the wall above her head and waited until her eyes lifted to his. "I leave the way I came."

She took a hard breath but held his gaze. For an instant, he was struck again by her determination and courage.

The back of his throat began to burn.

"Then I drive," she said without blinking.

"By all means." He pushed away and headed toward the open window, but then he surprised them both by returning to her and cupping her cheek. "I'm warning you now, Katarina. At the first sign of trouble, we abort. No questions asked."

"Whatever you say, Herr Reiter." The mutinous light in her eyes ruined any pretense of compliance on her part.

Jack sensed he was in serious trouble with this woman. He had to get matters back in his control. "One more thing," he said.

She angled her head at him.

"Make sure you dress warmly." He shifted to the window, dipped and then swung his leg over the ledge. "It's going to be a long, chilly night."

Chapter Six

The drive to Wilhelmshaven began in silence, and continued that way for most of the journey. Sitting in the passenger's seat, Jack surveyed the passing landscape. There was no horizon, no clear distinction between land and sky, just an inky blend of dark and darker. An occasional shadow slid out of the night, only to retreat as they sped by. Wind shrieked through the invisible slits of the car's windows.

Concentrating on the road, Kerensky drove cautiously, with both hands on the wheel. She hadn't looked at Jack since they'd left the city limits of Hamburg. Which was just as well. Between the poor quality of the road and the poorer quality of the car's headlights, driving required her undivided attention.

He took the opportunity to study her out of the corner of his eye. She was dressed head to toe in black wool. Black pants, black sweater, black gloves—the perfect ensemble for blending with the night. She'd slicked her thick, fiery hair off her face and twisted it into an intricate braid that hung halfway down her back.

He could almost feel the vibration of her carefully contained energy. Like a sleek, untamed animal poised for a fight.

She baffled him, tugged at him. She had a face meant for the movies and was so lovely his chest ached every time he looked at her. But he also knew how much depth lay below that exquisite surface.

Never once had he caught a hint of the corruption or selfishness that drove most spies. His instincts told him that she had her own personal agenda for working with the British. Those same instincts also told him that her motivation was connected to a dark secret she kept well hidden from the world.

He understood all about dark secrets and hidden motives, as well as the moral confusion that came from lying and stealing every day. For too many years, Jack had relinquished his Christian integrity—*no,* his very soul—to carry out other men's agendas. German. American. What did it matter if he was Jack Anderson, Friedrich Reiter, or someone else entirely? One face, two names, no identity. Those were the legacies the bureaucrats had created for him.

Now this woman, with her strength and determination, made him think beyond the mindless killing machine he'd become. She made him toy with the idea of a future beyond the war. He suddenly wanted something…more. More than hate. More than vengeance. Something that went beyond his own humanity.

Worst of all, the woman made him hope for a better world, where belief in God meant something beyond a faded memory.

This was the wrong business to feel emotions, *any* emotion, especially ones that made him soft toward a woman.

"You're too beautiful," he blurted out.

She whipped her head around so their gazes met in the dim light.

She gave a deep sigh of frustration before returning her attention to the road. "It's called *heredity.*"

Heredity. Right. The word tugged at a thought hovering in the back of his mind. Jack forced himself to remember he was having this conversation for her benefit. "Your beauty could be used against you." He'd seen it often enough.

"Or to my advantage. Lucky for you, there's more to me than a pretty face." She sounded weary, as though she'd given this speech countless times before.

Jack wasn't impressed. He was responsible for keeping them both alive. He had to be able to predict her behavior and gauge what she would do if she ended up in a crisis. "This mission depends on your quick reflexes and ability to think on your feet. For at least five minutes you'll be alone inside the *Kriegsmarine* headquarters."

"I'll only need three."

He did his best not to react to her bravado. "Wrong attitude. You can't be impatient. Impatient equals careless. And careless equals one dead female spy."

A nerve flexed in her jaw. "Have I given you the impression that I'm stupid?"

"One mistake is all it takes."

"It won't be mine."

She returned to clenching her teeth.

He returned to holding on to his temper.

"Fancy words, Kerensky. Will you be able to back them up?"

He didn't know her well enough to judge for himself. And for five long minutes he would be unable to control the situation, unable to protect her if Admiral Doenitz awakened. Jack knew she was hiding something from him. And he thought he knew exactly what it was. *Heredity.*

If he was right, the woman could not be caught. Ever.

He knew what they would do to her, where they would send her.

No emotion. He reminded himself of his personal motto that kept him alive. *Nothing personal.*

Who was he kidding? "How much Jewish blood runs in your veins?"

Her sharp intake of air was barely audible, but he'd heard it all the same. Already knowing the answer, he found himself holding his breath, waiting for her response to his bold question with a mixture of dread and hope. When she held to her silence, he wondered if he might have been wrong in his assessment.

Jack Anderson was never wrong. "How much?"

Her hands tensed on the wheel, the only sign of her agitation. Making a soft sound of irritation, she adjusted herself with a swoosh of wool against leather. "We do not speak of these things in Germany. We do not even whisper them in the dark confines of a car."

He had no easy response. She was right, of course.

Even if she was only part Jewish she could not reveal such a secret to him.

No emotion, he reminded himself again. *Nothing personal.*

"Consider the subject closed," he said.

She locked her gaze with his for a full heartbeat, two. Three. Then she began a very slow, very thorough once-over of him. Since the road ahead of them was long and straight, he sat perfectly still under her perusal. He owed her that much at least.

Eventually, she turned her head back to the road. "We're nearly there. Soon, this will all be a distant memory for us both."

Jack took a hard breath. He wished he could ignore the risks of going through the front door with nothing more than a loaded gun. This would be a good time for prayer, if he was still a praying man. "Are you sure I won't fit through the window?"

She snatched her eyes off the road, looked at his chest and then shook her head. "You won't."

Her voice sounded strong, confident, but she looked bleak. And her hands shook slightly.

Was she having second thoughts? Had he thrown her off balance by accusing her of being a Jew?

He knew touching her was a bad idea. *Don't do it,* he told himself. *She is not a harmless female. Not this one.*

He ignored his own warning and reached out, lightly fingering a lock of hair that had come loose from her braid.

She took a shuddering breath.

He dropped his hand. "I don't like the idea of sending you in there alone."

Her shoulders stiffened and all signs of her distress disappeared. "We've been through this already. I'm going into that room, end of discussion."

"What discussion?" he muttered.

She flipped him a smug look. "Exactly."

"Careful, Kerensky." Jack jammed a hand through his hair. "You're treading on razor-thin ice with me."

She bared her teeth. "Good thing I'm light on my feet."

"You're a difficult woman."

"So I've been told." She cleared her expression and pointed ahead of her. "Look up there, on your right. The harbor."

In the next instant, before he could stop her, she swung the car down a dark alley and cut the engine.

The night swallowed them, pitching the interior of the car into blinding darkness. A hot, nagging itch settled in his gut.

Unable to make out anything other than a heavy nothingness, Jack squinted into the eerie gloom. Still… *nothing.*

A sudden blast of anger left his nerves raw.

It was too dark. Too remote.

Too isolated.

He'd allowed Kerensky to park the car facing toward the back of the alley. If an ambush awaited them, there would be no getting out alive.

Very, *very* stupid.

He touched the panel in his sweater where he'd sewn

a cyanide pill into the stitching. Trained to choose death over revealing secrets, Jack Anderson knew his duty. He'd seen men with stronger convictions break. He'd seen innocent men break, too. Jack would not join their ranks. Too many lives were at stake. The Nazis could never be allowed to get to the information he had stored in his head.

Suicide was the only solution. His own damnation was well worth the lives he would save with his permanent silence.

Tonight, however, there was a woman's life at stake. He would make sure the choice between disclosure and death never happened. Jack would do what he must to ensure the cyanide pill made it through another mission unused.

"Turn the car facing out," he said, his voice flat and hard.

"What?"

"Either do what I say, or I do it myself."

"I…" She shifted in her seat, then sighed. "Of course. I wasn't thinking." Her voice held a slight shake, as though she'd stunned herself with her thoughtless behavior.

Another act? Or was she still upset over their conversation about her "heredity"? Upset enough to make a mistake in the admiral's room, as well?

Before he could question her, she started the engine and put the car in gear. Jack stayed planted in his seat as she made quick work of the direction change.

Once she threw the brake, a thin bar of light from a nearby streetlight slid across the front of the car's hood.

Better.

"Do you want to go over the hand signals one last time?" he asked, relief making his voice softer.

"No." She cut the engine again, tapped her temple two times. "Got it all in here."

Jack plucked the keys out of her hand before she could pocket them.

"What are you doing?" she growled.

Hardheaded, inflexible, full of pride. Did everything have to be a battle with her?

"You can't carry these with you." He jingled the keys in front of her nose. "Too much noise. And if you're caught or hurt or any number of possibilities, I'll need to be able to drive the car out of here."

She opened her mouth to argue. Again.

He merely looked at her.

Her snort was quick and full of wounded pride. "It must be quite a burden, being perfect all the time."

"You have no idea."

"Humble, too."

He ignored her goading. "Details are the most important aspect of any mission. Forget just one and a man *or*—" he gave her a meaningful look "—a woman will end up dead before there's a chance to rethink the situation."

"So you're the detail man." A statement, not a question.

Jack allowed himself a smile. "For better or worse, Kerensky, tonight we're a team. You might as well accept it."

And so should you, he told himself, as he tucked the keys underneath the driver's seat. "Let's go."

Nodding, she picked up the black knit cap sitting on the seat next to her and began tucking her braid into it. Her eyes took on the excited gleam of a child's at Christmas. "Curtain up."

Such eagerness to get the job done, such conviction. I remember feeling that once, a lifetime ago, Jack thought.

Where did my convictions go? When did they go? The answer was simple enough. The day the Nazis sent the real Friedrich Reiter to kill him.

Lord, he started to pray, then cut himself off. This was a time for action, not a time for useless prayer that would bring no immediate help to the mission.

Jack gave Kerensky a sharp nod. "Let's go."

As one, they climbed out of the car and snapped shut their respective doors without making a sound.

A few steps and the cloak of the alley's gloom lifted. Icy damp air hit Jack's face as it sliced off the sea. Sand and wet leaves waltzed around his ankles and clung.

Kerensky repositioned her hat. Jack took a moment to check his weapon, a 9 mm Luger P08—the most effective German handgun available. He examined the magazine, a simple eight-round in-line box, and then clicked the safety mechanism in place.

Kerensky's eyes lingered on his gun's tip. "Do you really think that's necessary?"

"You don't?"

She took a steadying breath. "I—"

"This isn't make-believe, Katarina. And I won't give

false assurances. Get that straight right now. Bad guys with guns are out there." He hitched his shoulder toward the harbor.

Dragging her eyes away from his weapon, she looked at him dead-on. "And you always go in prepared. Is that it?"

"Exactly."

She didn't argue the point further. "I understand."

He placed a hand on her shoulder. "No heroics. We abort at the first sign of trouble."

"Right."

Without another word, she turned on her heel and set out at a clipped pace. Jack let her walk exactly three steps before he reached out and stopped her again. "Remember, Admiral Doenitz will be in that room tonight. Sleeping. We do this quietly."

The intense green eyes that met his were level and clear. "I'm a cat. He won't know I'm there."

As she headed out again, Jack went into automatic mode. He memorized their route. Keeping the harbor always on his left, buildings on his right.

Stop. Gauge. Check bearings. Move on.

Again and again, he kept to the pattern as Kerensky wove them toward their destination. She led him along six streets, each thirty-eight strides long. On the seventh road they moved onto an open sidewalk lining a small park, passing four squat, identical stone buildings.

Kerensky stopped moving at the corner of the eighth street. She looked to her left, then to her right. Darting across an alley, she flattened against the closest wall.

Motioning with two fingers, she indicated the building

on her left. The two-story structure was made of color-less granite and stood guard over the drab waters that led into the North Sea.

Closing the distance, Jack mouthed a warning. *No mistakes.*

Grimacing, she clamped a hand on his arm and folded him deeper into the shadows with her. She then gestured to the impossibly small window above their heads. Silently measuring the dimensions, Jack admitted to himself that she'd been correct. He'd never fit through the tiny opening.

Unfortunately, she would.

No second chances. No margin for error.

No turning back.

The mission was under way.

Chapter Seven

Although the stingy moon gave a mere suggestion of cold, pale light, Katia could still make out the expression on Friedrich Reiter's face. Grim. Resolute. She didn't need much imagination to know he considered her completely unsuitable for the task that lay before them. She could practically hear his mind working, gauging, assessing.

She couldn't fault him for his skepticism. With his unexpected question about her Jewish blood, he'd nearly thrown her off balance enough to make her as inept as his silent accusation claimed.

How could he have guessed her secret? And in so little time? Had she given herself away? The thought scared her beyond reason and she experienced an irrational urge to cry. With one simple question, Reiter had turned Katarina Kerensky into an amateur.

And now Friedrich Reiter had all the advantage. Which was too deadly to contemplate.

Remembering her mother, and all they had to lose

if Katia allowed anyone or anything to distract her, she
pulled out her most effective weapon—a sultry smile.

Reiter's expression remained implacable.

The man was a rock, the personification of cold, chilly
calm. Katia could probably learn from his technique. In
fact, next to him, she felt like a bit player in a second-rate
theater company.

As he continued to stare at her with unyielding eyes,
her stomach flipped inside itself. She rubbed a hand over
her belly, afraid the knots were there to stay.

At least for the rest of the evening.

Tapping his watch, Reiter pulled her attention back
to the mission. He held up five fingers, silently reminding her that he would give her no more than the allotted
time to get the job done once she was inside Doenitz's
room.

She inclined her head in a brief nod.

A corner of his lips lifted in a sarcastic twist as he
made a stirrup with his hands and crouched low. When
she hesitated, he elbowed her to get moving.

Sighing, she kicked off her shoes, planted one foot
in his cupped palms and placed her hands on his wide
shoulders. For a second longer she merely stared into
his eyes. In that beat of silence, something unnamable
passed between them. Something that sent a shiver of
foreboding up the back of her neck.

This man was not like the rest. He was pure danger,
yet he was also a man she needed on her side.

Acutely aware of the hard muscles bunching under
her fingertips, Katia was instantly reminded of her vulnerability, that she carried a dark secret underneath all

the layers of acting and subterfuge. For a brief moment, she had the dangerous sensation of wanting to lean her head on those broad shoulders and let Friedrich Reiter carry her burdens for a while.

A normal reaction, she told herself, considering the stress she was under and the unwanted reminder of all she had to lose. Still, she had to stifle any further weakness—especially of the feminine kind—if she wanted to concentrate on the job she had to do.

Tonight there could be no mistakes.

At Reiter's impatient grunt, she shoved off the ground and pivoted in his hands. With a quick push, he lifted her toward the windowsill above her head.

Fully exposed now, the wind slipped icy fingers of cold and wet below the neck of her sweater. The breath rushed out of her lungs, but she steadied herself by flattening her palms against the wall in front of her.

Breathe, Katia. Focus on one task at a time.

Unable to see much in the dim light of the moon, she used her sense of touch to guide her. Careful to keep her movements slow and silent, she clung to the ledge with one hand, tested the latch of the window with the other. The rough metal gave way under her gentle push.

Luck was finally on her side. She knew Reiter would scoff at the sentiment. He didn't seem like a man who would rely on anything other than cold, hard logic.

She could use some of his sharp focus right now. It was times like these she just wanted...out.

But then what? Leave her mother in Germany, in the clutches of a man like Hermann Schmidt?

Unthinkable.

Convinced once more, Katia pushed the window forward another few inches, gripped the ledge with both hands and pulled herself up.

Precise and whisper quiet, each movement made with careful purpose, she inched past the windowsill. One last push from Reiter and she was through the window. She twisted midfall and landed on the floor with a soundless thud.

The window slid shut behind her.

No turning back now.

Blinking, she did a quick visual scan of the room, but was unable to see past her nose. She debated whether to take a step forward or wait in frozen immobility until her eyes adjusted to the darkness. Choosing the latter, she put her other senses to work.

Her ears picked up soft snoring coming from the other side of the room, slightly to her left. The scent of salt and sea and musk filled her nose. The smell wasn't unpleasant, exactly, just…strong.

As the inky gloom turned to a muted gray, Katia slowly reached to her left. Her hand connected with a large dresser. She blinked several more times, finally able to distinguish the dark shapes of the furniture from the shadows cast throughout the room.

She flicked a glance to her right, counted two additional, smaller dressers. A washbasin was perched on a table off to her left. The expected bedside table sat next to a small bed that contained a lump buried under a blanket.

Doenitz.

The sight of the sleeping admiral had her shifting a

couple inches to her left. Caught between impatience and fear, her natural reflex was to rush her steps in order to get away from the man as quickly as possible. But she forced herself to think of Doenitz as a nameless, faceless blob, rather than a decorated admiral with enough power to kill her on the spot if he awoke.

She wondered if she would feel this strong aversion to him if she didn't know who—and what—he was. Now was not the time to ponder such a question.

One minute down.

And counting.

The floor beneath her stocking feet sparkled in the dim moonlight. Someone had obviously taken the trouble to polish it on a regular basis.

Admiral Karl Doenitz was as fastidious as the rumors claimed.

It was a good reminder for her to touch nothing or, at the very least, to put everything back in its precise place if she did.

Edging closer to the bed, she saw that the key ring was exactly where she'd been told it would be.

Her source was as reliable as ever.

Unfortunately, the intelligence hadn't been complete. She'd expected to find just one key, not four—*four!*

One minute, thirty.

Regardless of the ticking clock in her head, Katia took ten full seconds to simply stare at the key ring. *What now?* She didn't have enough wax to make an impression of all four keys. Nor the luxury of confirming her choice with the actual cabinet containing the plans.

That left her only one option.

Guess.

Doenitz chose that moment to grumble and shift in his sleep.

Katia dropped to her knees and melted into the shadows. As the cold heat of fear slammed through her, the air clogged in her throat, making it difficult to take a breath.

Turn your fear into action, she told herself. *Fear into action.*

Ah, but the fear wasn't going to settle so easily.

At least Reiter was just outside the window. The thought made her feel more confident. Safer.

She could do this.

Swallowing, she concentrated on slowing her heartbeat and waited patiently for Doenitz to relax back into his snoring.

After several very long, very tense seconds, the admiral's breathing found its rhythm again. On her hands and knees, Katia scooted forward and around to the right side of the bed. Reaching above her head, she clamped her fingers over the cold metal key ring.

Taking a quick inventory, she discovered that three of the keys were long, thin, with identical rounded tops. Just like...house keys?

The fourth was shorter, and fatter than the rest, just like—dare she hope—a cabinet key.

Yes. She nearly offered up a prayer of thanks. If she thought God was listening, she might have.

Instead, she dug in her pocket, pulled out the small box containing the special wax. Flipping open the lid with her thumb, she lifted the entire ring of keys and made the impression.

Three minutes down.

Careful to avoid making any sound, she set the keys back on the table and fanned them out in the same order as she'd found them.

Box in hand, she let out the breath she'd been holding. Backing slowly toward the window, she turned around at the last second and realized the window was too high for her to reach without assistance. She lifted her hands above her head, but found no ledge to use.

A chair sat just to her left, but was perched at an angle that wouldn't do. One small pull, a quick readjustment and the angle of the chair was right at last. Seconds later she was up and through the window, tumbling straight into Reiter's arms.

His warmth enveloped her.

Before that moment, she hadn't realized how cold she'd been inside Doenitz's room. Insanity overrode logic and she snuggled into Reiter, pressing her cheek against his broad shoulder. She took a shaky breath.

For a ghastly second, she wanted only to stay in the shelter of his arms. Her fingers flexed against his chest, then relaxed.

His hard breathing was unmistakable, and she wondered if he was battling emotions anything close to the ones she was fighting.

She turned her head to look at him directly. His eyes, unblinking and very, very close, lit with a question. She lifted the box she still clutched in her hand, and then grinned like a fool.

He smiled down at her, his expression softening just enough to have her wonder if he had a bit of human blood running through his veins after all.

Before she had a chance to ponder the thought, he dumped her to the ground and tugged her around the corner. She barely had time to catch her balance and pocket the wax impression before he shoved her from behind. "Go, go, go."

She took off running in the direction in which they'd traveled earlier. One foot in front of the other. Legs pumping fast. Feet pounding faster. Cold wind slapped her face.

Run. Run. Run.

She heard Reiter closing in behind her, protecting her. The sensation gave her the courage to pick up the pace.

Three blocks later, he pulled her to a stop and yanked her into the shadows with him.

Handing her shoes back, he blessed her with a look of satisfaction. His smile gleamed in the moonlight.

He wasn't even breathing hard.

"Well done," he said. "You made it with a full minute to spare."

Still panting, she closed her eyes against an over-whelming desire to bask in his praise. "Nerves of steel."

A lie if ever she'd told one. A bead of sweat trickled along her hairline, a sure sign of the stress she was trying to hold at bay.

She forced her breathing to slow, clamping down hard on the string of hysterical laughs trying to bubble out of her. Madame Levine would be pleased with her control.

At the thought of her former mentor, Katia's joy disintegrated. Would her mother be sent to a camp, as well? Would Schmidt figure out their secret, as Reiter had done so quickly in the car tonight? What if the U-boat captain already knew? What if he had his own plans for them, plans that included a trip to the camps?

There was so much at stake, so much to lose. So much—

"We're not safe yet," Reiter reminded her.

Fear scrambled to the surface. "I…I know."

If they were caught now, all their planning would have been for nothing.

What if Katia was caught tonight? Would the Gestapo come for her mother—not because of her secret heritage, but because Katia had tried to fight them?

Elena would suffer unfairly for her daughter's actions. Was she risking too much by helping the British? But what else could Katia do? God had long since taken His hand off Germany while too many sat back and did nothing. As a result, Hitler's power had reached unstoppable proportions.

A surge of fear shimmied along the base of her spine.

She would not panic. She would not panic. She would not—

"Stay focused, Katarina." Reiter took her chin in his hand and gave her a long, measuring look. "Concentrate on one thing at a time."

"Yes." She swallowed. "Of course."

"Let's get back to the car," he said.

"You have to let me go first."

"Right." He dropped his hand, his expression as unreadable as always. "Stick close."

"Like glue."

He took two steps then stopped and turned back to her. "No. I have a better idea."

With a casual shrug, he wrapped his arm around her shoulder and gently tugged her next to him. The gesture sealed them into a single unit. Subtle. Powerful.

Unnerving.

Katia struggled to think over the wild drumming of her pulse. She hadn't felt this safe since her father died. She distrusted the sensation completely. "What are you up to?"

His slow smile oozed charm and sophistication, creating an intimacy between them that quite simply scared her to death. It was then she realized what he had planned.

"From this moment on, we're a couple."

Under the circumstances, the tactic made perfect sense.

"We need to make this look good…" He lowered his voice to a caress. *"Darling."*

"I'm the trained actress," she reminded him. "Watch and learn from the professional."

She then gave him the kind of smile that usually scrambled men's brains.

He lifted his eyebrows in response. "Perhaps a bit obvious, Katarina. But you have the right idea."

"You want obvious?" She batted her eyelashes at him, and then trailed a fingertip along his jaw.

They stared at one another awhile longer, each breathing heavier than the situation warranted, but then they both laughed. The spontaneous gesture added the right touch of lightheartedness to the scene.

To an outside observer, they looked like two lovers sharing a long night of, well, whatever their imaginations wanted to dream up.

Playing it for all it was worth, Reiter continued looking at her in the way a man looked at the woman he loved.

The swift ache of loneliness came fast and hard. Reality came faster.

This was a ruse, she reminded herself.

They were spies. On a mission. Nothing more.

Get it straight, Katia.

"Lead the way, Herr Reiter," she said in a perfectly steady voice.

"By all means."

They walked arm in arm for three full blocks, the perfect picture of romantic bliss, but as they rounded the last corner, Reiter slowed his steps. And then...

The unmistakable grind of a hammer sliding into place rang in her ears.

"*Halt!* Or I'll shoot."

Chapter Eight

Jack froze.

Right here, right now, what he did next would determine all of their fates. His initial instinct was to turn and fight. But he made himself slow down, think offensively, and consider other options first.

Anticipation shimmered along his skin, tightening his muscles, making him more aware, more alert. And ready to strike. A quick hit to the three vital points—throat, nose, temple—was all it would take.

It would be so easy to succumb to impulse. Friedrich Reiter would have no qualms over killing a guard.

Jack Anderson wouldn't either, if it meant protecting the woman beside him. But Jack also knew better than to make such a rash mistake.

The Germans were meticulous record keepers. Once the guard was found, a report would be made. The grounds would be searched. And before long, Kerensky's little uninvited jaunt into Doenitz's room would be discovered.

The mission would be over before it had really begun.

The rhythmic sounds of Kerensky's breathing reminded him of her presence. This was why he preferred to work alone. What if she was captured and interrogated tonight, what if she got hurt in an escape attempt, what if…

No. *Think in terms of absolutes,* he told himself, *not ifs.*

He would do this right. With cold, hard pragmatism.

No emotion. Nothing personal.

And, lo, I am with you always…

Jack nearly flinched at the unexpected thought. Where had it come from? An old Scripture memorized from youth, or a reminder straight from God?

Jack couldn't be certain. So he focused on the only reliable sources he had at his disposal. His brain. And his skills.

Without moving, he took note of the line of fog snaking along the waters of the distant harbor. The vapor would eventually shroud the entire town in its milky-white mist. Perfect cover for escape.

"Get your hands in the air." The order was spat in clipped, rapid-fire German. "Now."

In one part of his mind, Jack counted off seconds. The rest of him searched for a solution that would keep all three of them alive. Measuring, gauging, he dropped a quick glance on to Kerensky. She met his gaze with hard steel in her eyes.

Good. She wouldn't buckle.

"Do it, or I'll shoot," came the order. The voice was angry and a little desperate now. Jack knew from personal experience that desperate was the same as reckless.

Just what they needed—a desperate, reckless Nazi with a loaded rifle pointed at their backs.

After giving Kerensky's shoulder a brief squeeze, Jack lifted his hands in the air above his head. She took a hard breath and did the same. By his calculation, less than fifteen seconds had passed since the guard's initial command to halt.

"Turn around," came the next order. "Slowly."

Jack slid another glance at Kerensky. Her eyes were narrowed into determined, pale green slits surrounded by spiky dark lashes.

"We do this together," he whispered.

She nodded. "Together."

As a unit, they pivoted to face the enemy. For a split second, time came to a standstill and the world waited for one of them to make the next move.

Jack took a quick accounting of the guard. Dressed in a *Kriegsmarine* uniform, the rank of midshipman was evident by the single bar on his shoulder strap. The sailor was shorter than Jack, slighter and much, much younger. Nothing more than a boy, really.

A boy who carried a 98 Mauser infantry rifle, with its five-shot clip, and simple, strong action that could pierce a man's—or woman's—heart at this close range with little to no mess.

Not the best of situations.

But not disastrous, either. As long as Jack kept his head thinking and his emotions shut down.

"State your name and your business." The voice was still strong, firm even, but the sailor's eyes reflected hesitancy, as though he sensed Jack's superior rank in spite of the civilian clothing.

Easing into the role of authority, Jack brought his hands to his waist. Palms facing forward, he took a deliberate step forward and addressed the sailor by his official rank of sub-lieutenant. *"Fähnrich zur See—"*

The rifle jerked. "Get your hands back where I can see them."

Jack knew exactly what he had to do now. A plan began formulating in his head. Placate first. Stall. But, at all costs, avoid bloodshed.

He took another step forward, careful to keep from spooking the guard any further.

However, Kerensky—the careless, rash woman— chose that moment to join the conversation. "Oh, honestly, this is ridiculous," she said, lowering her hands slowly, but without an ounce of hesitation. *"Fähnrich,* there must be some mistake. Although, I'm sure it's nothing we can't work out."

The sailor's eyes narrowed. "Do I know you?"

Jack recognized the curling in his gut as a mixture of anger and fear. He'd almost had things under control. Why hadn't the woman kept her mouth shut?

"Let me handle this," he hissed at her, his eyes burning with silent caution that only an idiot would ignore.

Kerensky, of course, chose to disregard the clear warning. Why he'd expected any differently was a mystery to him. With a flick of her wrist, she yanked off her cap. Her braid tumbled down, down, down, landing in a soft thump against her back.

Holding back a string of oaths, Jack took another step forward, shifting to his right, until he stood between her and the guard.

The sailor's face went dead-white as he craned his neck to look around Jack. "You... You're Katarina Kerensky."

So much for anonymity.

She pushed Jack aside and gave the sailor one of her brilliant smiles. "Why, yes. Yes, I am."

Wonder of wonders, the boy's shock turned into immediate adoration, and the rifle's nose tipped toward the ground. Well, well. Kerensky was using her fame to dazzle the kid. Rash, yes. Careless, most definitely. But maybe, just maybe, workable.

"I grow weary of this silly game," she said.

Jack agreed completely.

The gun tipped lower still. Another minute and the rifle would be Jack's.

"Yes, I, that is, I thought you were a threat."

"A threat? Oh, you can't be serious." She let out a tinkling laugh and tugged her braid over her left shoulder. Twisting the tip around her finger, she managed to look feminine, frivolous and very nonthreatening.

From the glint in the sailor's eyes, it was clear the boy felt genuine embarrassment over the incident. Jack wouldn't have believed it if he hadn't seen it for himself. Even through the haze of his frustration, he knew the wisdom of letting the woman play out the charade to the bitter end.

"*Fähnrich*—"

"My name is Franz Heintzman, Fräulein Kerensky."

"Well, Franz…" She looked up and smiled into his eyes, all grace and charm in the gesture. A fairy-tale princess come to life. "You don't mind if I call you by your first name, do you?"

"I'd be honored."

"You see, Franz," she continued. "My, uh, friend and I were taking a stroll along the quay for some fresh air after…well…" She flipped her braid back over her shoulder and left the rest unsaid.

The sailor blinked. "But why here in Wilhelmshaven?"

Kerensky leaned forward, crooked her finger at him until he drew closer to her. "We wanted privacy this evening. I—" she straightened, reached out and clasped Jack's hand for a brief moment "—or rather *we*, don't want others to know of our liaison just yet."

Jack actually heard the kid swallow. It was all over now. Battle lost. Surrender inevitable. He almost felt sorry for the boy. Almost.

The power of the woman was amazing, mindboggling. Jack didn't know whether to tap her on the back in admiration or wring her pretty little neck for taking such a risk.

"Yes, yes, I think I understand," Franz said. Then he looked at Jack again, the earlier suspicion in his eyes replaced with unmistakable envy.

Kerensky had been wrong about one thing. Her beauty wasn't a weapon. It was mass destruction.

As though sensing his silent awe, she gave Jack a quick smile then pivoted back to the sailor. "Franz, dear, perhaps we could keep this incident our little secret?" She circled her hand in a gesture that included all three of them. "Maybe pretend you never saw us here tonight?"

Clearly wavering between doing his duty and making friends with a famous actress, the sailor looked from her to Jack and back to her again. "I'm not sure I can do that."

Kerensky turned him facing toward the harbor and hooked her arm in his. "Let's talk plainly, shall we?" Lowering her voice, she created an intimacy between them that had the boy blinking rapidly. "I really don't want anyone to know about my visit here, for obvious reasons. What would make this easier for you?"

"Well, I don't suppose—" He stopped and looked everywhere but at her.

"Yes?" She patted his hand, blessing him with a look that had his Adam's apple bobbing in his throat.

"I have a two-day leave next week. And, I would really like to see your latest play."

"Done." She went on to explain where he could pick up his ticket, adding a promise to meet him backstage—in her dressing room—after the performance.

At the excited beam in the boy's eyes, Jack had seen enough. It was long past time to end this farce.

Kerensky was no longer star of this show. Jack was.

Drawing alongside her, he gave a brief smile to the midshipman. Then, in a perfectly reasonable tone, he said, "Darling, it's getting late. We should be on our way."

Instead of arguing with him, wonder of wonders, her eyes filled with relief. "Yes, yes, of course."

Not one to miss an opportunity, Jack took immediate advantage of the woman's startling cooperation. With his mind on escape, he eased Kerensky closer to him, while offering a quick farewell to the boy.

Jack waited just long enough for Kerensky to say her own farewell before wrapping his arm around her shoulder and steering her in the direction of the car.

Although the guard had fallen under Kerensky's spell quickly enough, Jack knew their luck wouldn't last. German military training was too strong, too thorough. It wouldn't be long before the boy came to his senses and took them to his commanding officer for questioning.

Jack picked up the pace.

Chapter Nine

Three minutes and two blocks later, Katia let out a deep sigh of relief. Surprised at the need to rest in Reiter's protection a little longer, she had to resist the urge to retreat farther into the safety of his casual embrace.

For one, they weren't alone. She sensed rather than saw the sailor's presence still behind them, watching. Waiting. Perhaps even wondering if he'd made the right decision in letting them go so easily.

She wanted to look over her shoulder, but Katarina Kerensky *never* looked back.

Instead, her eyes shot to Friedrich Reiter's face. His expression was impassive, his steps slow and lazy. She wasn't fooled for a second. She could feel the tension slicing through him. His entire body may have looked relaxed, but there was no doubt in her mind that he was wound tight, ready to attack if the need arose.

The thought was as comforting as it was disturbing.

She knew he could have taken out the sailor in a matter of seconds, but something had held him back from killing the young man.

Had it been a deep sense of morality? Or had he simply been maintaining the integrity of the mission, ensuring no signs of their presence were left behind? A dead or injured guard would have been an unmistakable calling card.

One they would not have been able to take back.

Swallowing hard, she felt unusually restless and uneasy. Perhaps it was because she knew so little about the man walking beside her. And yet, she trusted him completely.

Odd. Katarina Kerensky trusted no one except herself. A Scripture came to mind, one her father had taught her during the dark days of revolution. *But they that wait upon the Lord shall renew their strength; they shall mount up with wings as eagles; they shall run, and not be weary...*

Because the verse had brought her father great comfort, Katia had memorized it, as well. Along with his other favorite verse, *My grace is sufficient.* Even in his last moments, Vladimir Kerensky had never lost faith in God.

Could Katia ever trust the Lord again, like she had as a child thanks to her father's righteous example? After years of relying on her own strength, she doubted it would be as easy as making a decision on a cold night in Wilhelmshaven.

Still...

Hope and bitterness warred within her. She didn't know whether to laugh or cry, to surrender to the Lord or continue in her own strength like always. Up to this point, she'd done well on her own.

But now?

Now things were…different.

And she feared the man walking beside her had everything to do with the change.

She needed time to think, to sort through her confusion, but they weren't safe yet.

"We better make this look real," she whispered. "I'm sure our new friend is still watching."

"Excellent idea." Reiter stopped, turned her until she faced him directly. The intensity in his gaze made the air hitch deep in her lungs. She couldn't bear the way his eyes searched her face, but she was too mesmerized to look away.

"Our man's less than fifty yards behind you, on your left," he said, leaning down to touch his forehead to hers. "We have to get this right the first time."

"You don't need to worry about me. Let's not forget who just saved whom."

He pulled back and rewarded her with a quiet smile. She decided his quiet smiles were the most dangerous. "Gloating, are you?" he asked.

"Absolutely." She leaned into him, blinked like a cowering fool, because, well, why deny the truth? She wanted him to kiss her. And wasn't that incredibly shocking?

His grin never faltered. In fact, to the untrained eye, he looked completely smitten with her. If Friedrich Reiter needed a career after the war, the man could make a fortune on the stage.

Dropping his head until their noses were an inch apart, he waited a beat. "I'd expect nothing less from you."

He was making her nervous, and that made her angry. Not to mention incredibly afraid of losing control. She tried not to bristle, but temper mixed with confusion and fear twisted into a hard knot in her stomach, and had her wishing for a little more privacy. So she could kick him in the shin. "Why do your compliments always sound like insults?"

His expression softened. "Just part of my charm."

"Of course."

Watching him closely, she didn't move, didn't breathe. An eternity passed before his lips touched hers. They pressed, retreated, pressed again. A moment passed, then another. By the third, her knees gave out and she stumbled into him.

"Well done, that should convince him," he said as he helped her find her balance, then set her at arm's length.

His voice sounded too steady. Too sure. How could the man remain that unmoved when her own legs were literally giving way under the weight of her reaction to their short, meaningless, pretend kiss?

She had to cling to his shoulders to keep from tripping into him again.

He gave her an odd look, almost sad. "Let's not overdo it, Kerensky."

With a few quick maneuvers, he tucked her under his arm again, and led her toward the car.

"Our man just left," he informed her.

"I know."

Needing distance, she took a step away from him, but he tightened his grip on her shoulder and pulled her back against him. "He could come back," he explained at her questioning stare.

"Right." But how was she supposed to calm her scrambling pulse when he wouldn't let her have room to breathe?

Enough was enough. She was through being the only one off balance. "I saw your look of shock when I started talking," she said. There. That should get an interesting reaction out of him.

For the first time that night, his steps faltered. "Shock doesn't begin to describe it."

"Oh?" She smiled sweetly at him, fully aware that she was baiting the human equivalent of a wild animal. What was the old saying about pulling a tiger by his tail? Did the same apply to cougars?

"Try frustration, anger, sheer terror for your safety. That sailor had his full attention on *me,* which is exactly where I wanted it. What I did not want," he said as his voice filled with reproach, "was him noticing you."

She was starting to get seriously insulted. "As if I can't take care of myself," she muttered.

"By revealing your true identity? That's how you take care of yourself?" He blew out a frustrated breath. "It's a wonder you're still alive."

"But I am. And so are you. Thanks to me, I might add."

"What happens if your name shows up in a report, Katarina? Did you think about that when you were playing the famous actress out for a little tryst with her... friend?"

"Revealing my identity made it more believable. You'd

see that if you'd look past your colossal ego. Let's say my name does end up in a report, so what? All it will say is that Katarina Kerensky and her unnamed friend decided to come to this obscure little village to avoid stares. My idea was just short of brilliant."

"If you do say so yourself."

"Weren't you the one who said you wanted us to appear as lovers, in case someone saw us?" She gifted him with a smug grin. "But, no, wait, you were too busy thinking like a soldier back there, instead of a regular man."

His eyes, a deep, troubled blue that had judged her just minutes before, now looked…weary. "All right, you have me there."

She stared at him, her eyes going wide in spite of her attempt at playing nonchalant. "You admit it?"

They rounded the corner to the alley and he made a grand show of opening the car door for her. "Haven't you ever met a man who can admit when he's wrong?"

"Actually, I haven't," she said as she lowered herself to the seat.

He scooted her over with his hip and then settled in next to her. "Then let me be your first."

Having a man, especially such a large man as Friedrich Reiter, sitting this close to her made the inside of the dark car seem too crowded, too confining.

Blinking at him, she shifted farther across the seat, but when he dug the keys out of their hiding place, she froze. "Shouldn't I drive again?"

"No. You need to get some sleep. But before you settle in, let me have the box." He opened his palm to her.

Too exhausted to argue with him, she slipped the wax impression into his hand without a word.

After pocketing the tiny box in his jacket, he turned his attention to starting the car and steering out of the alley.

Once they were heading toward Hamburg, Katia busied herself with watching the passing scenery. Dark clouds drifted in odd patterns across the sky, converging in front of the moon and plunging the landscape into an eerie darkness. Apprehension slithered up her spine, making her shudder from the weight of the sensation.

A still, small voice whispered a warning in her mind.

Something didn't feel right about tonight, something she couldn't quite name. Not just the incident with the guard, but something else entirely, something to do with the mission.

Had she missed another important detail?

Trying to remain calm, she ignored the odd shivers dancing along her skin. But the sense of foreboding wouldn't go away.

Worrying was useless. So, she forced her mind to run through every detail of her time in Doenitz's room. The initial entry, dropping to the floor, making the impression of the key, her swift exit, the...

Oh, no!

No, no, no, no, no.

How could she have been so careless? In her haste to get out of the room, she had moved the chair to a slightly different angle below the window.

She'd exited quickly, quietly and, what she had thought

at the time, efficiently. Only now did she realize that she'd left the chair out of its original position.

After all her planning and all her posturing, she'd made a second mistake in so many days. They would have to abandon the mission now.

She needed calm. She needed strength, the same strength her father had tapped in to in his final days in Russia. *They that wait upon the Lord shall renew their strength; they shall mount up...*

No, wait. She was allowing the stress of the evening to do her thinking for her. She'd only left the chair marginally out of place. No one would notice the shift in its position unless specifically looking.

Friedrich Reiter had done this to her. With his dead-on suspicions about her Jewish blood and *pretend* kisses, he'd made her doubt herself and her abilities. He'd made her think she wasn't in control of her own destiny, when she'd been just fine on her own for years.

She'd never failed to complete a mission successfully.

She would prevail in this one, too.

Admiral Doenitz would never discover her tiny mistake. She was almost sure of it.

Chapter Ten

21 November 1939, Wilhelmshaven
Kriegsmarine headquarters, 0630 hours

Before his anger turned into an uncontrollable fit of rage, Admiral Karl Doenitz needed to cool his temper. It was, after all, his duty to remain calm in front of his men. Walking would help, but at the moment he couldn't find a decent patch of floor to pace across.

Feeling caged, he wove through the maze of humanity in his private quarters and went back into his office. Even here, members of his handpicked staff inspected every inch of the room.

They'd been searching for over an hour, but had found nothing missing, nothing out of the ordinary. Except, of course, the chair.

Breathing slowly, deliberately, he worked his hands at his sides, flexing, relaxing. Flexing, relaxing.

Someone would pay for this.

Blowing out a hard breath, he stalked back into his

bedroom and stared at the chair still sitting at its slightly awkward angle under the small window opposite his bed. Air wheezed out of his lungs, clogging his throat until he had to gulp for a breath.

Someone had actually infiltrated his private living quarters of the BdU, in spite of the increase in guards. In spite of the added precautions with the recent move.

The question was why? And why hadn't anything been taken?

Doenitz detested espionage and the intrigue that came with it. Just two months into the fight against England and this war already had more than its share of both. Nevertheless, he would adapt.

BdU Admiral Karl Doenitz *always* adapted.

With clipped steps he returned to his office and picked his way to the window behind his desk. Looking beyond the fishing vessels riding at anchor, he focused on the mouth of the harbor. A sharp wind gusted off the North Sea, frothing the dark waters with ragged whitecaps.

Shifting his focus to the U-boat pens peppered along the entrance, a swell of pride overwhelmed the other emotions raging inside him. Military duty was his calling. But the sea was his home.

Karl Doenitz was the *Kriegsmarine*. His U-boats were the first line of offense in the Führer's bid to seize power throughout Europe.

This break-in was an irritant that must be dealt with swiftly. He had to discover precisely what the intruder had been after. Only then would he turn his full attention back to the war with Great Britain.

Did one have to do with the other?

Nothing else made sense.

The British actually believed they could cope with the German U-boat threat. They were wrong, of course, and must continue in their misguided thinking. The strength of the U-boats and their advanced weaponry must remain secret.

Doenitz strode to the cabinet that held maps, plans, strategies and codes—all the weapons that would propel the Fatherland into the greatest power the world had ever seen. Stooping to study the lock, he ran his finger along the outer rim. The cold, smooth metal warmed under his touch.

As he continued to consider the lock, he caught a flicker of movement to his right. Rising, he turned to face Captain Emil Kurtz, his chief of staff. Even at this early hour the man glistened in the service suit required of all administrative officers. Doenitz took note of the immaculate blue uniform tailored to perfection and nodded in approval.

With perfect military precision, Kurtz saluted. "*Heil* Hitler."

Doenitz returned the gesture. "*Heil* Hitler."

"The search is complete, Herr Admiral. We've found nothing missing."

Doenitz's anger reared at the news. He coated steel over the emotion. "Any signs of tampering?"

Cool, composed, Kurtz's eyes cut from the cabinet back to Doenitz. "None, except the misplaced chair."

Doenitz nodded, his mouth firming into a determined line. The intruder had been careful, but not careful enough. The chair proved that much. One mistake always led to another.

He and his staff were simply missing the obvious.

As though reading his mind, Kurtz asked, "Do you want us to continue searching?"

"Make another sweep. In the meantime, I want to review the individual reports of each man on watch last night."

"Yes, Herr Admiral. I will get them to you right away."

"I also want to speak with every guard, personally."

Kurtz nodded. "I will arrange it at once." Eyes flat with concentration, he added, "We will find the intruder."

Certainty swelled. "I have no doubt."

Oh, yes. They would discover the identity of the guilty party. If not this morning, soon. Patience was the key.

Instincts honed in the heat of battle warned Doenitz that this was only the beginning.

The intruder would be back.

And Admiral Karl Doenitz would be waiting.

At exactly 0638 hours, Jack carefully checked for suspicious activity and, finding none, he bound up the front steps leading into the *Vier Jahreszeiten* hotel.

The historic building was a palace of old-world elegance. Never let it be said that Friedrich Reiter didn't know how to travel in style.

Ignoring the luxury of the gold filigree and yards of brocade-covered furniture, Jack strode to the front desk and obtained his room key. After a friendly, albeit brief, conversation with the sleepy-eyed clerk, he headed toward the staircase and to his suite on the third floor.

Jack had no doubt the clerk would make a note of his comings and goings. The report would further validate the charade of a man sneaking out for a clandestine meeting with his lover. He'd begun the act at the theater last night. Katarina Kerensky had added another layer to the ruse in Wilhelmshaven. Like it or not, Jack had to continue playing out his part.

With that loose end neatly tied up, Jack set his mind on blissful solitude, food and a hot shower, not necessarily in that order.

He took the steps two at a time, mentally reviewing the events of the last few hours.

For several obvious reasons, he would prefer not to continue his association with the famous actress. For one, now that Jack had the wax impression, he wasn't sure he needed her on the mission anymore. Not to mention the fact that he didn't trust aggressive females with fancy eyes and brave attitudes.

Who was he trying to convince?

Katarina made him remember the Godly man he'd once been. She made him want to search his mind for Scriptures he'd buried there as a child. Verses such as *The Lord is my strength,* and *We know that all things work together for good to them that love God.*

For two years, Jack had thought little of God or His word. Tonight, the Lord had been in his head every step of the way. Long-forgotten Scriptures had come to mind, seemingly out of nowhere.

Was the Lord trying to tell him something?

Jack was too short on sleep to know for sure. He needed to focus on the mission right now.

He would think about God later.

Unlocking the door to his hotel room, he glanced at his watch—0640 hours.

He'd been in Germany less than twelve hours, but that didn't mean his presence had gone unnoticed.

He began a systematic search of the suite, checking his subtle detection devices for signs of tampering. Starting on his right, he circled the perimeter in a counter-clockwise direction. The single strands of hair, each placed over knobs of closed doors, were still intact, as were the invisible slices of tape over random drawers.

Patrolling past the sitting room, he moved into the bedroom, explored the adjourning bath, and then went out onto the balcony.

He'd found no signs of unwanted entry or tampering.

Relaxing his shoulders, he turned and looked out over the city. Fog, wet and gray, slithered over the buildings in a glossy haze. There was an eerie post-dawn quiet as the morning cold swept in off the water and slapped him in the face.

Restless now, Jack was unable to enjoy the beauty of Hamburg. He strode back into the sitting room, shutting the balcony door behind him. Sinking into a large, overstuffed chair, he let the tension from the evening's events drain out of him.

It was only a matter of time before the SS contacted him. Friedrich Reiter was too important to Heinrich

Himmler's personal agenda for his return to Hamburg to go unnoticed for long. Jack would be ready.

At the thought of facing Himmler again, he felt a familiar rush of emotion surge through his blood. Guilt, he wondered? Or conviction. He wasn't sure anymore. He'd long since lost his moral compass.

He closed his eyes against the thoughts colliding into one another in his mind. Kerensky had slipped past his well-honed defenses, tapping into the man he'd once been. And now he couldn't stop thinking about all he'd lost that long ago night when he'd first met the real Friedrich Reiter.

Jack let out a harsh breath.

He would never forget the exact moment he'd stared into the eyes of his assassin, a Nazi secret agent who had come to kill him and assume his identity. The physical similarity between Jack and Friedrich Reiter had been uncanny. No, terrifying.

When Reiter had pulled the knife, Jack had had little choice but to defend himself. The fight had been long and brutal. The ending nasty.

Murder, self-defense, whatever word was used to describe what had happened in that back alley, a man was dead because of Jack Anderson.

Absently, he shoved at his hair, as though the gesture would rid him of the dark memories sliding through his brain and tangling into a knot of regret. Would the guilt ever go away? Would he ever look at his hands and not see the blood?

What was a man capable of when he stopped feeling guilt? Jack feared he was close to finding out. He'd become that embedded in his life as a spy.

He hadn't started out cold and unfeeling. When he'd decided to become Friedrich Reiter he had believed he'd been called to a higher good. He'd vowed to risk his life for innocent blood, as many other warriors had done in the Old Testament. He'd accepted the killing—not murder, killing—as part of the job. No different than a police officer.

MI6 had been more than willing to aid his quest. With special training, forged documents and the addition of a slight Austrian accent to his otherwise perfect German, Jack had literally turned into the man who had come to kill him.

The transformation had been so complete Heinrich Himmler himself believed Jack *was* Friedrich Reiter. Short of checking dental records, there was no possible way of telling Jack's real identity.

The line between Friedrich Reiter and Jack Anderson had begun to disappear. Until tonight. While looking into Kerensky's eyes, Jack had remembered the man he'd once been. And now, Scriptures learned long ago were coming to mind.

Trust in the Lord with all thine heart; and lean not unto thine own understanding. In all thy ways acknowledge Him, and He shall direct thy paths.

The Scripture was a powerful reminder of where Jack should put his faith.

Yet how could he acknowledge God in the travesty that had become his life?

Deception was a rotten business. He'd learned quickly

that he could trust no one. As a result, he'd become a hard man. Cynical. Faithless. All necessary to stay alive. The moment he became complacent, he became vulnerable.

Take tonight, for instance. He knew he should have never kissed Kerensky. Regardless of the need to present the impression of intimacy, the reflex to pull her into his arms had been too fast, too strong and entirely too powerful to deny.

What had been glorious one moment now haunted him.

Nothing personal. No emotion. Who was he kidding?

He bolted out of the chair and started pacing through the room. Hovering on the brink of emotions too dangerous to explore, he turned his attention to less frustrating matters of reports and organization.

Taking action, he set a record on the phonograph. German walls had ears, Hamburg walls more than most. As soon as the poignant strains of a Wagner opera filled the air, Jack went in search of the radio components he'd camouflaged inside the actual construction of his suitcase.

As he crossed into the bedroom, he checked his watch again—0655 hours.

On a small table near the window, he spread out a power lead, adaptor, aerial wire, connection cables, dial and Morse key. Working quickly, efficiently, he connected cables and made a mental list of the information he would transmit to the British.

He draped the aerial wire over the dresser, connected

the Morse key and dial tuning it to the prearranged frequency.

Using his personal five-digit series of codes, he made initial contact with the Brits, waited for the go-ahead to continue.

As was true of all agents, Jack's Morse style was as unique as his fingerprints. If the Germans happened to discover he wasn't the real Friedrich Reiter they could very well try to force him to continue transmitting wrong information.

Their efforts would be to no avail, of course. Jack would simply pause an extra beat after every word that started with *T* or *O,* thereby alerting the British he'd been compromised.

A minute passed. And then another. Finally, Jack received the go-ahead from London.

With cool precision, he tapped out his message in the prescribed code that would be translated before landing on his superior's desk then sent on to Churchill himself for review.

ARRIVED OKAY STOP
MET BUTTERFLY STOP
PHASE ONE COMPLETE STOP
BEGINNING PHASE TWO OVER

Per standard operating procedures, there would be no response until 1430 Hamburg time. Jack took apart the radio and returned the components to their original hiding places.

He peeled off his sweater, loosened the top button of

his shirt, and then pulled out the small cardboard box from his pants pocket. Flipping open the top, he studied the impression Kerensky had made of the cabinet key. Clear, precise. She'd done an excellent job.

But what if the plans weren't in the cabinet anymore? After the mistake she'd made over the change in location of Doenitz's headquarters, Jack couldn't trust the woman's intelligence.

He needed a backup plan. His best possibility would be to make contact with someone on the inside of Doenitz's staff, preferably someone who worked in the main building of the *Kriegsmarine* headquarters, a naval officer, someone who...

Schmidt. Of course. The U-boat captain engaged to Kerensky's mother.

A plan began formulating. When Jack had left Katarina this morning, she'd reminded him that she was to spend the rest of day with her mother and Schmidt. Jack had promised to find her later in the evening, after he'd had the key to Doenitz's cabinet made. However, now he would make sure they met much sooner.

With just the right amount of maneuvering, *Kapitän zur See* Schmidt could very well give Jack invaluable intelligence, without ever knowing he'd done so.

The tactic was a long shot, at best. Certainly dangerous, and would probably come to nothing.

But this was war. Jack had to take the risk.

Chapter Eleven

Katia used a heavy hand on her makeup. Not out of vanity, but to cover the consequences of her sleepless night. Friedrich Reiter might have thought she'd dozed during their ride back to Hamburg, but in truth Katia had spent most of the time wondering whether or not to confess her mistake in Admiral Doenitz's room.

Ultimately, she'd chosen to remain silent on the matter. At this point, what was done could not be undone. Yet, even as she tried to convince herself she'd made the right decision, a stab of guilt snaked through her stomach and she rose from her chair with a feminine growl on her lips.

She should have trusted Reiter with the truth. She knew that now. Nothing could be gained from withholding such an important piece of information. She must tell him the next time they met.

Satisfied with her new decision, she snatched her brush off the dressing table and moved to the closest window on her left. With an uncharacteristic lack of grace, she began yanking at the knots in her hair.

Tugging, tugging, tugging, she stared at the scene in front of her with unblinking eyes.

Sunrise over the rooftops of Hamburg made a magnificent picture, one she usually stopped to appreciate. But as Katia continued brushing her hair, she barely noticed the ribbon of golden light threading between the orange-and-red-tinted spires.

And then, after a painfully hard yank, a wave of despair crested inside her.

She was in too deep.

She wanted out.

But she couldn't leave. Not with her mother in such obvious danger.

Overwhelmed with too many emotions to sort through all at once, she admitted the truth to herself at last. Katarina Kerensky, a jaded woman who'd long ago lost hope, desperately wanted to believe good would overcome evil in the end.

Even after witnessing her father's senseless murder, even after accepting that the Nazis were in charge, Katia wanted—no, she *needed*—to believe that God hadn't abandoned the German people altogether.

God?

Where had that thought come from? She didn't believe the Lord cared anymore. Or did she?

My grace is sufficient.

Was it? Could she trust in the Lord again? Was there enough of Vladimir's daughter still in her to take that leap?

She wasn't sure. How could she put faith in a God who allowed a man like Hitler to rise to power?

She was just overly tired this morning. That had to explain her desire to rely on anyone other than herself, especially an invisible God.

Her mind wasn't working properly. She was confused over her mistake in the admiral's private quarters, stunned by her strange reactions to her new partner. Surely that explained her leaning to set aside her disillusionment and put her trust in a silent God.

The loud knock on the door made her jump. Happy for the interruption, she took a deep breath and checked the time. Her mother and fiancé were a full twenty minutes early for their scheduled outing with Katia.

Moving back to her dressing table, Katia studied her reflection in the mirror. She looked too haggard, too world-weary for the part she must play this morning.

Breathing deeply, she took a long, slow blink. The gesture wiped away the creases of worry on her brow. Another blink settled a vacant look into her eyes. A quick sigh, one last shudder, and finally she became the royal princess with little on her mind beyond the superficial. "Much better."

She thought she was back in control. Until the minute she opened the front door and the cold wind slapped ice-edged fingers against her face. Forcing a silly smile on her face, Katia braced against the frigid attack and took in the sight of her visitors.

Dressed in a cashmere coat made in her signature color of soft blue, Elena Kerensky stood arm in arm with her fiancé. Both held themselves proud and precise. But where Elena's arrogance came from her royal breeding, Schmidt's haughtiness had a sheen that was equal parts brutality and condescension. On closer inspection, his tailor-made *Kriegsmarine* overcoat looked like the work of Wilhelm Holters, the premier tailor of the Third Reich.

Nothing but the best for this Nazi.

Katia hid her cynicism behind a little sigh of plea-sure. "Mother. Hermann. What a lovely surprise. You're early."

"I'm afraid I was the eager one," Elena said. "I so want you to get to know Hermann better."

She lifted an adoring look at her companion and squeezed his arm. Schmidt smiled down at Elena with similar admiration. But Katia thought she recognized a look of cunning flash in his eyes.

Did he sense Elena's secret? Did he have a dark plan already in place?

Before Katia could pursue the frightening thought, Schmidt turned his bold scrutiny on to her. "May we come in? Or are we to stand on your doorstep all morning?"

The man was, beyond question, the most arrogant Nazi Katia knew. And considering the company she kept, that was saying a lot.

Tread carefully with this one, Katia.

Hidden beneath several layers of foolish woman, she cocked her head at an agreeable angle. "Oh, dear, forgive me. Do come in."

She moved to her left, blessing them both with a happy smile as they passed by.

Once inside, Schmidt turned on his heel and handed

Katia the bouquet of roses he'd been holding behind his back.

"For you," he said. "I understand they are your favorite."

He held her stare with a challenging look in his gaze.

Katia remained expressionless, fiercely so, but her mind raced in frantic chaos.

She hated white roses. No, she *detested* them. They reminded her of happier days when her father would bring a bouquet to both her and her mother for no particular reason.

Elena knew of Katia's aversion. Why would she allow Schmidt to make this cruel gesture?

A test, perhaps? But who was running the show, Schmidt or her mother? And was Katia supposed to react with outrage or complacency?

To avoid revealing her confusion, she quickly took the bouquet and buried her nose in the blooms. The scent made her stomach churn in anguish and a sense of loss besieged her. How she missed her beloved father. His faith had been strong, even in the moment of his death.

In comparison, Katia's faith was weak, practically nonexistent. But she was growing weary of relying only on herself and her quick thinking. *They that wait upon the Lord shall renew their strength.*

She swallowed her trepidation. "Thank you, Hermann. They're very beautiful."

"Go put the flowers in water, darling." Elena patted Katia's hand, the gesture reminiscent of when she had been a child with a hurt that needed soothing. "Then we'll leave for our outing."

At the odd note of apology in her mother's eyes, tears pricked at the back of Katia's eyes. What was Elena trying to tell her?

Unsure of the meaning behind the undercurrents traveling between them, Katia made herself breathe evenly. "I'll only be a moment."

Elena nodded, an obscure smile playing at the edge of her lips. "Good girl."

Ice clutched around Katia's heart. This secretive woman was not the mother she knew. Was Elena trying to tell her something? Something only the two of them would understand?

In an attempt to keep her hands from shaking, Katia concentrated on the task her mother had set before her. She filled a vase with water from the kitchen sink, all the while keeping her attention on her guests in the adjoining room. Thankfully, her home had an open floor plan.

As though staged by a seasoned director, Elena remained in plain view while Schmidt idly moved from one room to another. From beneath her lowered lashes, Katia traced his every step.

As he made his way systematically from one end of her house to the other, he ran his index finger along a table, a chair, another table. He craned his neck to look into a room off to his left, another on his right.

Clearly, he wasn't attempting to be subtle with his search. All the while Katia's mother simply watched him as though nothing was out of the ordinary with his bold inspection.

Were the two working together? Could Katia not even trust her own mother? A woman with far more to lose than most?

My grace is sufficient.

Even now, Lord? Are You in this room with me now? Or am I alone, like always?

"So," Katia said, forcing her fingers to arrange the flowers one at a time. "Where do you two want to eat this morning?"

"I think we should go to our favorite little café near the *Rathausmarkt,*" Elena said, turning to face Katia directly. "The Engel café. You know the one."

Katia caught the silent warning in her mother's eyes.

Sudden fear snapped to life, leaching into her muscles and nearly causing her knees to buckle. *Breathe,* she told herself. *In. Out. In. Out.*

But no matter how hard she tried to remain calm, the floor seemed to shift beneath her and she couldn't stop thinking about the danger her mother was in with her Nazi fiancé.

Swallowing, Katia moved back into the main living area and set the roses on a table near the door. "Yes. *Yes.* I adore the Engel café. I think that will do nicely."

Elena nodded at her in…approval?

Unaware of the silent communication between mother and daughter, Schmidt completed his final pass through the living room and stopped at Elena's side. His eyes held the same glint of fanaticism Katia saw in the most treacherous Nazis of her acquaintance. She had no doubt the kind of man Schmidt hid under the *Kriegsmarine* uniform.

The knowledge gave her an odd rush of confidence.

She knew exactly how to deal with monsters like this man.

If she was careful—and Katia was always careful— a relationship with Hermann Schmidt could prove valuable.

Besides, the more she kept an eye on the terrible man, the more she could keep a protective watch over her mother. One thing was certain, something wasn't right with Elena Kerensky.

Katia had to find out what.

"Now that I've put the flowers in water, why don't we leave for the restaurant?" she suggested.

Elena nodded at her again, her motherly approval as clear as glass this time. "Excellent idea, darling."

Gathering her handbag and coat, Katia forced her mind to work quickly. This was not the first time she'd been in a dangerous situation like this. In fact, she'd acted this role a hundred times, with a hundred different Nazis like Hermann Schmidt. The part fit her as well as the gloves she slid onto her hands.

But with her mother's involvement, the stakes had risen. Katia had to make this her most masterful performance to date.

Chapter Twelve

A band of low-flying clouds swallowed the last patch of sunlight, turning the Hamburg sky a stark shade of gray. Jack gauged the weather with the eyes of a trained sailor. Satisfied the rain would hold, he edged closer to the Engel café and studied the three diners through the large, plateglass window on his right.

The Nazi propaganda machine couldn't have staged a more perfect scenario. The handsome naval officer, dressed in all his military glory, dining leisurely with his two beautiful companions as though the war was already won.

But as convincing as the scene appeared on the surface, Jack knew first impressions were deceiving.

He shifted closer and instantly registered the odd stillness in *Kapitän zur See* Schmidt. Obvious mistrust glared in his eyes, eyes that never left Katarina's face as she chatted happily away. For her part, the woman had slipped into the role of silly daughter once again.

Jack's stomach churned with anger. Katarina Kerensky played a deadly game with a *very* dangerous man.

At least she had chosen a table directly in front of the window overlooking the town square. Her position put her in the line of vision of anyone who passed by the restaurant, including Jack.

It hadn't taken much to discover that Katarina and her mother frequented this café. Had Kerensky been expecting Jack to come looking for her? Was she worried about being in such an intimate situation with her mother and Hermann Schmidt? Perhaps her boast that she could "handle" the two had been nothing more than false bravado.

A protective instinct surged again, making Jack want to race into the café and snatch Katarina away. Away from men like Hermann Schmidt. Away from Germany. Away from anything that would put her in danger.

Jack shook his head.

What was wrong with him? Katarina Kerensky was no amateur. She knew the risks.

Jack feared for her anyway.

As if to mock his foul mood, the clouds split open and a ray of sunshine speared a path from him to the café. The added light gave Jack a better view of his surroundings. Leaning against a monument built to commemorate the Great War veterans, he checked the perimeter around the café before he moved into position.

Activity in the town square was down at this hour. A row of plants lined the walkway next to the restaurant, while a scatter of empty chairs peppered the deserted area under a faded green canopy.

Overhead, the spire of the St. Nikolai Church punched above the rest of the buildings, as if to proclaim its steadfast presence despite the surrounding evil. The church's intricate design outshone the ordinary Hamburg rooftops. There was a time in which Jack would have seen that as a sign of God's very real presence in his life, reminding him that he wasn't alone.

Draw nigh to God, and He will draw nigh to you.

Was it that easy? Could he simply turn to God and know he would be welcomed home?

Before, Jack would have answered his own question with a resounding yes. Not anymore. The day he'd become a spy had been the end of simple answers to hard questions.

Setting his mind back on business, Jack aimed his gaze on the interior of the café and studied Schmidt more precisely. Even from this distance, he could see that the German's eyes belonged to a warrior. When the Nazi wasn't glaring at Kerensky his gaze darted around the interior of the café, assessing each table.

Was he looking for something specific?

Or someone?

No doubt, the man had checked out Jack's background by now. He'd be stupid not to investigate Friedrich Reiter after the tension in their first meeting backstage at the theater. But again, Jack wasn't going to rely on supposition or visual perceptions. Now that he was here Jack needed to find out whether *Kapitän zur See* Schmidt was going to be a threat to his current mission.

No time like the present.

So do not fear, for I am with you...I am your God.

The fresh reminder of God's promise settled his mind. Pushing away from the monument, Jack sauntered toward the café. He didn't bother with stealth as he entered through the front door. Friedrich Reiter feared nothing and no one. Intentionally drawing all eyes to him, he wove through the crowded restaurant at a leisurely pace.

Disregarding Schmidt's glare and Elena Kerensky's worried lift of an eyebrow, Jack took Katarina's hand and brushed a kiss across her knuckles. "What a happy coincidence finding you here."

She lifted her gaze to his. For a split second, their stares connected with a force that nearly flattened him.

"Herr Reiter," she said. "This is a surprise." Her voice was filled with obvious pleasure.

Even knowing this was an act for her companions' benefit, Jack found himself swallowing. Hard. "A pleasant surprise, I hope."

"The very best." She practically purred.

Loyalties tangled and warred inside him. He was beginning to feel the stirrings of deep emotion for this woman. The kind of stupid feelings that got a man killed if he went in unprepared.

I am with you...I am your God. Jack smiled. A little.

Katarina blinked, slowly. "You remember my mother and her..." She motioned to Schmidt. "Friend."

With a grand show of reluctance, Jack shifted his attention to the couple across the table. "Of course."

"Please, won't you join us, Herr Reiter." Elena Kerensky motioned him to the empty chair at their table.

"Thank you." He settled into the offered seat and

studied Katarina's mother with open interest. She stared at him with equal boldness. Her eyes were filled with a hundred questions, but she held her tongue.

"I hope I'm not interrupting something important," he said solely to her.

"Not at all. We were just preparing to order." Her tone was affable enough, but there was obvious distrust in the stiff angle she held her shoulders.

She was reserving judgment. Smart woman.

Hermann Schmidt, however, had come to his conclusions already. He glared at Jack with disdain.

The naval officer must have discovered information about Friedrich Reiter that didn't sit well with him. Jack looked forward to finding out just what the other man had uncovered. It would be an opportunity to gain necessary information about his alter ego's growing reputation.

Relishing the upcoming confrontation, Jack smiled the smile of a predator.

Schmidt returned the favor.

Katarina looked from one to the other then cleared her throat. "Hermann was just telling me about his recent commission." She smiled at him. "Admiral Doniky himself gave the orders."

"Doenitz," Schmidt corrected with a large dose of annoyance.

She gave him a vacant look. "Who?"

"We just went through this, Katarina. Not Doniky, *Doenitz*. Admiral Karl Doenitz."

She sighed heavily. "Oh. Yes, that's correct. Doe-nitz. I don't know why I can't get that right." She turned her attention to Jack. "Isn't it amazing that Hermann knows a *real* admiral?"

She looked and sounded enthralled with the idea, but only in a superficial way. There was nothing of the spy in the woman now.

Impressed with her acting abilities, Jack smiled at her with an indulgent grin, the kind a man gives the woman he adores.

"And best yet. Hermann has promised to introduce me to the admiral tomorrow evening at mother's party."

Jack pulled her hand in his and laced their fingers together. "How lovely for you, darling."

He kissed her knuckles then swiveled in his chair so he could place a smile on Elena. "It must be quite an honor to have such an illustrious man attend your party."

Elena lifted an elegant shoulder. "The admiral will not be the first high-ranking official in my home."

Below her lashes she slid a warning glare in his direction, a look meant only for him. If Jack wasn't mistaken, she'd just told him not to press the issue any further at this time.

Jack went instantly on guard. Why would she make such a threat? Was Elena Kerensky the one he needed to worry about and not Schmidt? He gripped Katarina's hand a little tighter.

Elena looked down at their joined hands. "You will come to the party, Herr Reiter? As Katia's escort, of course." Her smile was sleek and polished and impossible to read.

Jack inclined his head. "I would like nothing more."

Katarina let out a sweet laugh. "Oh, lovely."

Schmidt brought his glass to his mouth, the gesture drawing Jack's attention. The officer took a long swallow and then set it carefully back onto the white tablecloth— a little too carefully. "Elena, darling, would you and Katarina be so kind as to find our waiter and tell him that we are ready to order?"

Elena opened her mouth to speak.

Shaking his head, Schmidt raised his hand to stop her. "I would like a moment alone with our new friend."

She looked prepared to argue but then stood abruptly. "Yes, of course, Hermann. Whatever you wish." She held out her hand to her daughter. "Come along, darling."

"Why do I have to go, as well?" With the perfect blend of surprise and hurt pride, Katarina furrowed her brow. She played her role well today.

"We need to allow the men a moment to speak privately," Elena explained.

Wide-eyed, Katarina looked from Jack to Schmidt to Jack again. He could only guess what the actress was really thinking behind the empty look she swept across him.

"But I want to stay with—"

"Come, Katia." With a firm hold on her arm, Elena all but dragged Katarina out of her chair. "We shall be back shortly," she said to Schmidt.

"*Very* shortly," Katarina added over her shoulder as she stumbled after her mother.

Schmidt waited until the women moved out of earshot

before speaking. "You are not the first man to succeed with Elena's daughter."

"I am fully aware that she is quite popular with men."

Schmidt's eyes turned mean. "Nor are you the second, third or fourth. She goes through them quickly."

Jack resisted the urge to hit the man square in the face. "Better and better. I won't have to teach her anything."

Seeing that his scheme wasn't working, Schmidt switched tactics. "Let us dispense of these verbal niceties, Herr Reiter, and get straight to the point."

Jack drummed his fingers on the table in a show of vast impatience. "And here I was having such fun."

"I know you are a rogue SS operative." Schmidt paused to sneer. "One of Heinrich Himmler's handpicked lackeys."

Allowing the cold, bitter shell of Friedrich Reiter to envelop him, Jack narrowed his eyes and put the entitlement of an SS *Sturmbannführer* in his manner. No one was allowed to question a major in the SS with such blatant insolence. *No one.* "You are well-informed. For a sailor."

The insult hit its mark, but Schmidt quickly hid his reaction behind a casual shrug. "I have my sources."

"Who are these sources?" Even his voice took on Friedrich Reiter's ruthless timbre.

"That is not important. What I want to know is how long the SS has been following me?"

Following him? "Why would we be interested in you?" Jack looked at his wristwatch and feigned boredom, but every cell of his being stood on high alert. "You are nothing more than a U-boat captain."

Schmidt pressed his lips into a firm line and refused to respond. But the damage had been done. Clearly, the man had a military secret the navy didn't want the SS to know about. He'd made a stupid mistake. The arrogant Nazi had no idea who he was dealing with.

But before Jack could begin his own subtle interrogation, the women returned to the table.

Soothed by Katarina's presence, Jack had to remind himself not to stare too hard at her. Something about the way she smiled at him, with that secret look in her eyes, mesmerized him. He couldn't take his eyes off her.

This was an act on both their parts, but one that made him want to rid himself of Friedrich Reiter once and for all. Katarina Kerensky made him want to forget his drive for revenge and recapture the man he'd once been. A simple naval engineer who loved his God and his country. In that order.

In fact, he wanted—

It didn't matter what he wanted. Jack Anderson's life was no longer his own. He was a man with blood on his hands. There could be no forgiveness for him now. No matter how close he drew to God, God would not draw close to him. Why would He?

Jesus came to save sinners, all sinners, a small, distant voice said in his mind. Was it just a memory from Sunday school? Or truth?

As though sensing his internal struggle, Katarina reached out and squeezed his hand. For one dangerous moment, Jack allowed a thread of hope to rope through his bitterness. He pulled her hand to his heart and held it there.

She flattened her palm against his chest and smiled at him, *really* smiled. "I took the liberty of ordering for you, darling." Her voice shook with emotion. "You will stay?"

He pulled her hand to his lips. "I am at your disposal."

His voice sounded raw in his ears. Something powerful was happening inside him and it scared him.

Katarina's smile widened. "Lovely."

They continued staring at one another and Jack found himself allowing his own smile to spread.

The gesture felt foreign.

Schmidt cleared his throat, drawing Jack's attention once again. "Now that that's settled. Why doesn't Herr Reiter tell us something about his life growing up in Vienna?"

Well played.

If Schmidt had done his research, and Jack had no doubt that he had, they both knew Friedrich Reiter spent very little time in Vienna. But by his condescending expression, he seemed to be buying the ruse that Jack was here to pursue Katarina for purely romantic reasons.

To be sure, it was always best to warn off a dog before the fight got ugly. Releasing Katarina's hand, Jack slid deeper into his role of SS henchman. For a brief moment, he allowed Schmidt to get a good look at the deadly fiend inside him.

To his credit, the naval officer didn't flinch. In fact,

Jack caught the flash of recognition in the other man's eyes. One monster appreciating another.

Hermann Schmidt was proving a formidable foe.

"Very well, *Kapitän*. Ask me whatever you wish."

No matter what question Schmidt threw at him, Jack already had the answer.

Chapter Thirteen

By midafternoon, a bone-chilling wind whipped through the Hamburg streets. Moments earlier, Jack had left Kerensky with her companions in the restaurant and then headed south toward the edge of town.

Friedrich Reiter had an unscheduled appointment to keep. One Jack Anderson had put off long enough.

Knowing his prey well, he took a direct route along the intricate network of canals that had inspired the city's nickname, Venice of the North. Every step he surveyed his surroundings with a well trained eye.

So far, the city had been untouched by war. Modern buildings stood shoulder to shoulder with the historic Baroque and Renaissance architecture that drew thousands of tourists to Hamburg every year. The city would not remain intact for long. The British were that determined.

Ignoring a twinge of remorse over the destruction to come, Jack put his mind back on his duty. Traffic was light at this hour, which made his surveillance of the area simple enough. He had chosen this specific route for a purpose. The SS needed to believe they had found him, rather than the other way around.

Enjoying the solitude while it lasted, he lifted his face to the sky and sniffed. Winter was nearly here; he smelled it on the harsh wind.

Barely ten minutes into his walk, Jack found himself in front of the St. Nikolai Church. While his mind had worked on the mission, his feet had brought him to this bold reminder of God's holy presence in a fallen world. But rather than feeling hope at the sight of the magnificent structure, a wave of regret washed over Jack.

As much as he wanted to walk inside St. Nikolai, maybe get down on his knees and pray, he could not. Like all SS officers, Friedrich Reiter had renounced his church membership years ago. Jack could not be seen entering a church building. For any reason.

Another wave of regret flooded his mind. It was only a matter of time before the Nazis rid Germany of Christianity completely. A new religion had already been created for the people, one based on blood, soil, German folklore and the Thousand Year Reich.

Germany was on its way to becoming a godless country. Pastors and priests who dared to preach the one true Gospel were being sent to concentration camps as quickly as the Jews. Soon all the voices of dissent would be silenced.

Lord, what can one man do in the face of such evil?

The cold silence that followed his question was answer enough.

With a heavy heart, Jack started back down the street.

He barely covered a full block when a sleek staff Mercedes pulled alongside the curb. The vehicle slowed to a crawl, keeping perfect pace with Jack's long, easy strides.

The SS had found him.

A block away from the St. Nikolai Church.

Jack turned his head slowly, leisurely, in time to catch a flicker of movement behind the glass. Eyes free of all emotion, he pivoted to face the car directly. From the backseat, a man in the black uniform of the Gestapo motioned him closer.

Jack's fingers curled into fists. Heinrich Himmler had come himself.

The head of the SS had personally contacted Jack only on a handful of occasions, when the situation required secrecy, stealth and Friedrich Reiter's sinister methods of warfare.

Himmler contacting his dark angel of death now, in broad daylight, meant something big was in the works, something that couldn't wait for the cover of night.

At that thought, an increasing weight of responsibility settled onto Jack's shoulders. He was in too deep. And no one would come to get him out.

He was alone.

Or was he? *I am with you…I am your God.*

Himmler rolled down the window with precise slowness and then skimmed his ice-edged gaze over Jack. "Get in the car, Herr Reiter."

Jack's skin grew slick with sweat, the icy sensation

slipping deep within his soul as though an arctic wind had swept through him. Dealing with a man like Hermann Schmidt was child's play compared to a confrontation with the head of the SS, second in power only to Hitler himself.

Squaring his shoulders, Jack climbed into the car, into the world of darkness and evil that defined Friedrich Reiter's existence.

"Herr *Reichsführer.*" Jack closed the car door with a snap. "I was on my way to you."

"How fortunate for us both I found you first."

Jack nodded.

The Nazi motioned to his driver to pull away from the curb, then fell into a long, cold silence. Watching. Waiting.

Jack held the other man's stare. In the stark light of day, Himmler looked more like an accountant than the head of the SS. There was a kind of exacting, almost efficient, strain in the way he held himself erect and unmoving in his seat. The irony that so much power lay in the hands of such a small, nondescript man never ceased to amaze Jack.

Although there was nothing terrifying or demonic in Himmler's general demeanor, Jack had witnessed firsthand a bloodless indifference in the Nazi's character that made the man pure evil.

Jack's stomach pitched and rolled. As Friedrich Reiter, one of Himmler's most vicious secret agents, Jack wore anger and hatred like an ill-fitting skin. Darkness clung to him, its talons reaching all the way to the place he'd once kept his conscience. He was out of his league with such unprecedented evil.

He feared he'd never come back into the light.

Never will I leave you; never will I forsake you.

Jack nearly jolted at the reminder of God's promise racing through his mind. He'd long since turned his back on the Lord. And yet, had God stayed with him all this time? Did God's mercy run that deep?

"Herr Reiter." Himmler cleared his throat. "We are obliged whenever we meet to remind ourselves of our principles—"

"Blood, quality and toughness," Jack finished for him, accepting the verbal test for what it was—a subtle, yet dangerous, interrogation.

At his immediate response Himmler nodded in appreciation. "We weren't expecting your arrival for another three weeks."

With the suspicion sitting thick and heavy in the air between them, Jack shoved his desperation to cling to God into a dark pocket of his mind and donned the ruthlessness of his alter ego.

Friedrich Reiter would show only brutal efficiency, and nothing but absolute loyalty to his revered leader. "The early arrival was driven by my latest mission for the British."

"Which is?"

The British knew that Jack had to reveal certain facts to the Germans while gaining more valuable information for the British. It was a nasty, tricky business that often ended in both sides losing. But the few gains the British did learn were well worth the price. Or so the new head of MI6 had declared at Jack's last briefing.

"I am investigating a German naval secret weapon. One the British believe is responsible for sinking their cargo ships at an unprecedented rate."

Himmler looked sharply at Jack from behind his pince-nez. The man had a sobering capacity for weighing the underlying agenda behind straightforward information. Unnerving, yes, but potentially useful if Jack stayed focused.

"Then it is as I suspected," Himmler said.

Jack lifted a single eyebrow.

"Admiral Doenitz has withheld information from me."

Friedrich Reiter was a mindless killing machine, trained to allow the SS to do his thinking for him. A brainwashing, of sorts. One founded on paranoia. "You don't trust Admiral Doenitz." It was an obvious conclusion Reiter would make.

Himmler released an ugly, twisted laugh. "I trust no one outside of the SS. The admiral, in particular."

And *that,* Jack knew, was true enough. Himmler's paranoia was mind-boggling, yet all too real. Just a few months ago, he had created a state within the state. By law, the SS was now separate from all other German agencies and loyal to Himmler's personal agenda alone. Jack feared this cold-blooded Nazi's reign of terror was only just beginning.

He thought of the motto engraved on Friedrich Reiter's SS belt buckle and ceremonial dagger. *SS man, loyalty is thy honor.* Such blind obedience could only result in unspeakable horrors.

Jack let out a snort of disgust and tapped into the role he was supposed to be playing. "Doenitz is of the old guard. His ways are dying."

"Agreed. But the admiral is claiming those British shipping losses are a result of his superior U-boats. His fleet is not yet that strong." A calculating expression flashed in Himmler's gaze. "This secret weapon the British want you to investigate must be the true hero, not the U-boats."

"It's what MI6 believes. And why I am here."

Silence fell between them.

But then Himmler's eyes narrowed. "The actress you were with at the Schnebel Theater last night, how is she involved?"

Although Jack had expected Himmler to find out about his association with Kerensky, he had to swallow the quick reflex to deny knowing her. The best way to protect the woman from the fanatical Nazi was to give the obvious answer. "No, Herr *Reichsführer.* My involvement with Katarina Kerensky is of a...personal nature."

He let the insinuation settle between them.

"Ah, very wise. A woman with her connections could be useful to you in the future."

"Precisely." But if Jack had his way, her connections would soon be severed, because she would be living far away from Germany. In England. Or, better yet, America. If Jack was correct and she had so much as a drop of Jewish blood, she must leave Germany immediately.

The Führer's "final solution" was an unspeakable horror that must be stopped. Barring that, escape to all those soon to be affected.

For the first time since becoming Friedrich Reiter, Jack's desire to end the Nazi terror went beyond simple revenge.

Perhaps he was growing a conscience once more. Perhaps his earlier thoughts of God were the whisperings of the Holy Spirit. Perhaps everything—the attempted murder, the becoming an agent—had been leading him to this point in time. Not to stop the monster regime for his own personal reasons, but for people like Kerensky.

And what better way to bring down the enemy than from within its ranks? Could good come out of this evil situation? Perhaps, if God was personally involved. This mission was too big for Jack to carry out alone. But maybe he wasn't alone.

Lord, I—

Himmler's voice jerked him back to the matter at hand. "Your visit is indeed timely, my friend." A terrifying display of obsession flashed in the Nazi's eyes.

Here it comes. The reason Himmler had sought him out this morning.

Jack shifted in his seat. "Tell me what you want me to do." He spoke in Reiter's uncompromising tone.

"I want you to find a way into the Krupp-Germaniawerft shipyard in Kiel, where they are outfitting a U-boat with a new weapon, the same one I suspect the British have sent you to investigate."

Jack held his anticipation in check. *This* was the value of his secret life, this gathering of information from both sides so that he could piece together a solution to help the British war effort. "As you wish, Herr *Reichsführer*."

"One last request, Herr Reiter."

Jack felt a chill run down his neck, but he held Himmler's unblinking stare.

"I want the information in less than twenty-four hours."

Jack released an almost vicious laugh. "You have great faith in my abilities."

"I have great faith in *my* abilities." Himmler set a black leather briefcase on the seat between them. "Open it."

Jack shot a quick glance at the other man, but Himmler's impassive eyes gave nothing away.

Staring straight ahead, Jack placed the case on his lap. With a steady hand, he released the latch and drew out two sets of blueprints. He ran his finger across the outline of the first. "A German U-boat."

"A brand new design for a U-boat, to be precise," Himmler said. "Type XB is the first of its kind. But there are two more on the way."

Jack's gaze flew across the page. His mind raced, absorbing details, memorizing the technical aspects of the submarine's structure that was so different from other U-boats. "I've never seen one like this before. There are only two torpedo tubes at the stern."

"A feature unique to the XB. You will also see a total of thirty shafts along here." Himmler dragged his finger to the other side of the drawing. "And here."

Jack did a quick calculation. "The dimensions are too

large for standard torpedoes." Which meant only one thing.

A new weapon. One that had been kept secret from the SS.

Himmler spoke Jack's thoughts aloud. "We believe the shafts were specifically designed to carry another type of weapon. Your job is to find out what that weapon is, exactly."

Jack nodded, scanning the blueprint with the eyes of the naval engineer he'd been before Reiter had come to kill him. He read each notation, then reviewed the overall proportions. "What's her weight, submerged and fully loaded?"

"Top capacity is 2,710 tons."

Jack released a low whistle. "That makes the XB the largest U-boat ever built. She must pay the price in diving speed and agility."

"Which, again, leads us to believe the XB was built for a different function than open warfare."

"And you want me to verify the nature of the secret weapon, nothing more?"

"That's all." Himmler's lips thinned into a tight line. "For now."

Jack flipped to the next set of blueprints. His eyes scanned the outline of the Krupp-Germaniawerft shipyard, focusing on the U-boat pens just north of the yard facing the Bay of Kiel.

"U-116 is in sub bay A-4, which is," Himmler stated as he pointed to a spot in the northeast quadrant of the yard, "here."

Jack held back a grin. With the blueprints of the XB

submarine and the Kiel shipyard memorized, the completion of his mission for the British would be easy.

Too easy.

Himmler must have another agenda for sending Friedrich Reiter to the Kiel shipyard.

Was it a trap? Had Jack somehow betrayed himself since his last visit to Germany? No. If that were the case, he would already be under interrogation at Number 8, Prinz Albrecht Strasse.

With one trip to Kiel, Jack could gain the information he needed to help the British formulate a countermeasure for the bombs. Success tonight meant he would not have to involve Kerensky in the mission any further. In that, at least, he could keep her safe.

Thank You, Lord. It was his first prayer in two years. Short, imperfect, but heartfelt.

Returning the blueprints to the briefcase, Jack pulled the top down and clicked the latch in place. For now, he would think only in terms of the offensive. "I will have your information by 2300 tonight."

"You realize, of course, there can be no room for error." Himmler smiled, very slightly and with just enough vicious intent to alert Jack to the Nazi's dark mood.

"There never is, Herr *Reichsführer.*" Jack returned the smile with equal intensity, his mind drumming up an image of Katarina's sparkling eyes as they'd last stared into his. "There never is."

Chapter Fourteen

Katia didn't relish the upcoming confrontation with Friedrich Reiter, especially after their strained lunch. Aside from the tension-filled exchanges he'd shared with Hermann and her mother, the British spy had boldly staked a claim on Katia. Katia, for her part, had played cheerfully along. A little too cheerfully.

She could try to tell herself that her behavior was all part of the cover they'd been building since the first time they'd met at the theater, but she knew better. A very real connection was building between them.

Unfortunately, Katia had not been the only one to notice. The interrogation she'd suffered from both her mother and Hermann had been long and tedious. Worn out from the experience, Katia considered turning around and settling into a hot bath. But this was not about her. She'd stalled long enough. She had to tell Reiter about her mistake in Admiral Doenitz's private chambers.

Resolved to face the worst, she headed up the front steps of the *Vier Jahreszeiten* hotel.

The late-afternoon wind blew bitter and harsh against

her exposed cheeks. Katia didn't mind the cold. She found the nasty weather appropriate for the situation.

Entering the lobby with her famous smile in place, she sauntered toward the heavyset clerk standing behind the reception desk. His balding head shone from the reflection of the lights overhead. The poor fellow stared at her with a mixture of shock and interest.

"Fräulein Kerensky." He bowed in a show of deference reminiscent of old Russia. "What may I do for you?"

The clerk's reverence might remind her of all she'd lost, but this was not the time for nostalgia. "I understand Friedrich Reiter is a guest in this hotel."

"That is correct." The clerk spoke with meticulous politeness, but his eyes began filling with questions. Questions his training prevented him from asking.

She pulled a man's leather glove out of her purse, a prop she'd borrowed from the theater this afternoon. With a flourish, she set the article on the counter. "Herr Reiter left this at my home last evening."

The clerk swallowed, his double chin jiggling from the gesture. "I… Yes, I think I understand. Would you like me to deliver it to his room for you?"

The part of a woman without morals was not one of her favorite roles. In fact, the real Katia, the one she hid under all the subterfuge and lies, was appalled by the shamelessness required of the role. But if she could use her talent for nothing else, she could use it to save innocent lives. Ultimately. She had to get past this German first.

She swallowed her apprehension, shoved the real Katia a little deeper in her mind, and went to work.

"I wish to return the item to him personally. You understand." She punctuated her statement with a sly grin. "Perhaps you wouldn't mind telling me his room number?"

"I cannot give out that information, Fräulein." The clerk dropped his gaze to his toes. "It is against hotel policy."

"Come, now, Herr—" she scanned his name tag "—Schroeder. Won't you bend the rule this one time? For me?"

She drew slow, mesmerizing circles along the glossy reception desk as she spoke.

Schroeder swallowed, his gaze riveted on her swirling finger. "Room 312," he said in a choked whisper. "But you didn't hear it from me."

She placed her hand on top of his pudgy fingers and squeezed gently. "Hear what?" Her tone dripped with syrup.

Stuffing the glove back in her purse, she aimed a quick wink at the clerk, and then made her way toward the elevator. His choked gasp was far more rewarding than applause.

Fully aware that all eyes were on her now, she tilted her nose at a regal angle. After pushing the brass button, she lifted her chin another notch. Because this particular role required unprecedented boldness, she didn't fidget, didn't look around, didn't make eye contact with the couple waiting for the elevator with her.

Although she had to share the small space with the

gawking duo, she pretended not to notice how they whispered back and forth as she settled in next to them. She thought she heard something about her loose morals. Katia stifled a sigh. They were obviously too polite or perhaps too conventional to make any comment to her directly.

Typical German behavior, she thought with a hint of bitterness. Never make waves, never question authority and always, *always* look the other way. Like so many in the Fatherland, the elderly pair had been too easily "brought into line" by the Nazis.

For one black moment, Katia wanted to turn and scream at the couple, to yell at them to open their eyes and stop the atrocities going on in their own country.

But what would be the point? Most Germans were, well, they were just so *German*. Her own mother included. When bad things happened to them or their loved ones, they turned the other cheek. Literally. Not out of obedience to the pacifism taught by Christ in the Gospel, but out of fear. And maybe even laziness.

How many times must they be slapped down until they rose up and rebelled? A hundred? A thousand? Or would they never rise up?

Would they simply adapt to the horrors around them, as Elena Kerensky seemed to be doing?

Feeling a great burden resting on her shoulders, Katia rushed out of the elevator at the third floor. She held her breath until she heard the soft swoosh of the doors closing behind her.

Alone at last, she took a deep breath and headed down the hallway, toward room 312. After only a few steps, however, she caught sight of her quarry exiting his room.

He ambled along at an easy pace. She wasn't fooled by the lack of urgency in his steps. Even from this distance, Friedrich Reiter radiated absolute power. He was a man in control of everything, and everyone, around him. Yet there was something else that set him apart. It took her a moment to understand what made him different. He carried none of the Nazi intimidation in his manner. At least not with her.

Odd she would notice that about him now.

He stared at her as he approached.

Her face heated in a blush.

A blush? When was the last time Katarina Kerensky blushed? Long before Hitler had risen to power.

Reiter stopped mere inches in front of her and raked his gaze over her in blunt appraisal. Although the gesture was beyond rude, arrogant even, there was something unmistakably soft in his eyes.

Captivated, she leaned forward but just as quickly pulled back. "We need to talk," she blurted out.

Feet splayed, hands clasped behind his back, the air around him crackled with impatience. He was clearly headed somewhere important.

"Perhaps another time," he said.

Gone were any signs of the cooperative partner in a shared mission. This was a man who worked alone, a man who needed no one's assistance. "But you don't understand. I must—"

"I said another time, Katarina." He linked his arm

through hers and began leading her back toward the elevator.

Caught off guard, she allowed him to turn her around but sanity quickly returned and she dug in her heels. "I haven't yet told you why I'm here."

"It will have to wait. As you can see, I'm on my way out." He looked meaningfully at his watch. "And you have other obligations this evening."

"No, the theater is dark tonight. And I don't have any—"

"What of your mother and her fiancé?"

He had a point. A very valid point. Although no specific plans had been made, Hermann and Elena would expect her company later. "This won't take long."

She tossed her hair behind her back and hurried down the hallway toward his room.

Reiter caught up to her in five strides. "Perhaps you didn't hear me correctly." He clamped a hand on her arm, his gentle touch at odds with the frustration in his gaze. "I said I was heading out."

"What's the rush?"

"As I said, I have to attend to some business tonight."

She didn't like the sound of that. "You will want to hear what I have to say first."

She shrugged away from him and continued down the corridor. "Ah, here we are." She tapped the gold numbers on the door in front of her. "Room 312."

He appeared to debate with himself before letting out a frustrated burst of air. "This better be good."

"Actually, it's rather bad."

A thousand words passed between them without a sound. "Another piece of information you forgot to divulge?"

His directness made her hesitate. But she'd come this far. She wouldn't back down now. "Can we at least do this inside?"

He rubbed a hand down his face, muttered something unflattering about obstinate females. "All right. But don't say a word until I tell you it's safe."

"Safe?"

"We won't be the only ones listening."

The Gestapo had wired his room with a listening device? Already? She hadn't expected this. But she should have. Friedrich Reiter, whoever he was, was not a man to go unnoticed in a place like Hamburg for long.

She needed to be careful with him. Very, very careful.

Pushing past the threshold, Katia made a slow, comprehensive sweep of the room. She noted the spotless tabletops, the shining fixtures and the rest of the perfect decor. It struck her as odd that nothing was out of place. Not even a stray newspaper. She opened her mouth to remark on his unusual neatness, but he stopped her with a finger against her lips.

Frozen like that, with him standing so close she could smell his spicy, woodsy scent, she simply stared at him. He stared back. Another moment passed, and then another. Their breathing fell into a shared rhythm.

Her head grew dangerously light.

All the fear she'd told herself she didn't feel, all the tension she'd denied for days, came crashing into her.

For one insane moment she wanted to trust this man. She wanted him to share her burdens for a while. She wanted to tell him about her heritage.

She would not, of course. For one, the deadly secret was not hers alone.

"Katarina, *darling*." As he lowered his hand from her lips, the warning in his gaze cut like a blade. "What a surprise to see you…."

He trailed off, pointed to a table on her left, the telephone on her right and then up to the ceiling.

Three listening devices in this room alone? Someone wanted to keep a close eye on the man.

Nodding her understanding, she settled into her role. "You left your glove at my home last evening."

"And you couldn't wait to get it back to me, is that it?" His voice sounded amused, but his eyes were deadly serious.

"Something like that." For the benefit of the secret police listening to them, she continued talking in a soft, almost coy tone. She might hate this role but she played it well. "Or perhaps I simply missed you."

He gave her a very masculine chuckle in response. "Ah, darling. What fun you are."

He took two long strides toward a table, then fiddled with the dial of a modern-looking radio until the strains of a Wagner opera crackled in the air between them. *Tristan and Isolde*. Another story of star-crossed lovers. How…appropriate.

"Why don't you come over here and show me just how much you missed me."

She knew her duty, knew it was important to be

obvious. She also knew she could very well be heading straight to her doom with this man.

"I thought you'd never ask." She forced out a carefree laugh through very tight lips. No one would believe Katarina Kerensky had to work at this, not even Katia herself.

He turned the volume up a notch, and then kissed her on the...

Forehead.

The gesture was so sweet, and so at odds with the routine they performed that Katia's knees nearly gave out.

"Well." He kissed her again. On the forehead. Again. "That's certainly a nice beginning."

She started trembling, but so did he. For different reasons, she supposed. She could all but feel the impatience vibrating out of him, the frustration at being detained.

Or was it something else that made his hands flex and then relax at his side?

A vague sense of hope shot through her at the thought. She was on dangerous ground with this man, potentially life shattering. She had to remember this was an act for them both.

"I can do better," she said.

This time his chuckle came out low and slightly amused. "Please do."

But he didn't move toward her. The kiss, then, was up to her. She released her breath very slowly, very carefully. No one knew the importance of playing this role with practiced skill better than Katia. Swallowing one last time, she set her hands on his shoulders and lifted onto her toes until her lips gently touched his.

She drew quickly away. "Something like that?"

"It's certainly better than the first." His eyes filled with a challenge. "Why not try that again?"

The air knotted in her throat. She could do this. Of course she could do this. Lifting up again, she touched her lips to his for a second pass. Like a clichéd heroine in a Hollywood movie, she had to cling to him to keep from falling backward. "How was that?" she rasped.

"Much better."

His gaze filled with genuine affection. But in the next instant his expression closed, making him look as if nothing had happened out of the ordinary. The man was a rock.

Stone-faced, he gestured for her to follow him out onto the balcony. She wanted to rage at him for his coldness. She wanted to demand he show some emotion, any emotion. But she knew she wouldn't voice any of her thoughts aloud. The man was a professional spy. And so was she.

This was not a time to lose her head over a man, especially a dangerous one like Friedrich Reiter.

This was a time to take control.

Chapter Fifteen

Head high, determination firmly in place, Katia left all weakness in the room behind her and walked past the double doors leading onto the balcony. At the same moment, the big round sun dipped below the flat line of the horizon.

Utter darkness would soon descend over the city.

"Remember to keep your voice down," Reiter said.

She managed a tense nod in response.

Leaning back against the rail, he stretched his long legs out in front of him. The gesture made him look like he had endless time on his hands.

They both knew better.

"What was so important that it couldn't wait until later?"

Now that the time had come, she couldn't find the words. She hadn't expected her dignity to be so difficult to swallow. Glancing past him, she took a moment to gather her thoughts. Katarina Kerensky was not used to making mistakes. Admitting to them came hard.

"Katarina?"

Sighing, she shifted her gaze back to Reiter's. In a rush of whispered words, she told him everything, concluding with the exact angle of the misplaced chair.

He said nothing. Nor did he move. But she could see him pulling back from her, distancing himself mentally.

"Well?" she prompted.

Five long seconds ticked by, and still, he kept silent.

She dug her nails into her palms. "Do you have nothing to say?"

When he continued looking at her, completely unresponsive, with that unreadable glint in his gaze, she had to resist the urge to reach out and shake him.

But then...

Realization dawned. "You knew," she said. "You already knew."

"Not precisely. But from your conduct in the car this morning, I sensed something had occurred."

Hot tears of frustration stung in her eyes. All this time, he'd suspected something had gone awry and yet he hadn't said a word.

Was he that much of a gentleman? Or that much of a fiend? "I'm rendered speechless."

His lids drooped over his eyes. "Indeed."

She wanted to hate him for his casual behavior, but instead she found herself admiring him for his ability to remain calm in spite of his obvious anger.

He tried to push past her, but Katia grabbed his arm before he could leave the balcony. He looked down at her hand. She quickly released him.

"What do we do now?" she asked.

"We?"

"I'll do whatever it takes to put things right."

"You've done enough. Now, if you'll excuse me." He did not leave the balcony right away. Instead, he leaned against the doorjamb and gave her an impatient lift of a single eyebrow.

He was dismissing her.

Understandable, given the circumstances. If their roles were reversed, she'd react the same way. The wise response on her part would be to trust this British spy to finish the job on his own.

But could she trust him? This man she'd only met the night before?

The obvious answer was *no.*

Time was running out, not only for this mission but for everyone, including the British. England had suffered unprecedented losses from the Nazi secret weapon they were investigating, half of which were merchant ships carrying much needed supplies. If the British Isles were cut off from the rest of the world, England would fall to Germany. And if England fell, who would rise up to stop Hitler?

Katia could not put her trust in anyone other than herself. With a man like Hitler at the helm of Germany, the stakes were too high. "We don't know the mission has been compromised," she whispered.

"It doesn't matter. The moment you left that chair out of place was the moment you became a liability."

"Not necessarily. I can find out the extent of the damage tomorrow night, at my mother's party when the admiral arrives."

His jaw tightened. Clearly, he was having a hard time holding on to his patience. "We can't wait that long. Our options are dwindling. But if I leave now I may still be able to salvage this mess."

"Wherever you're going, take me with you." Desperation made her voice come out shrill.

"Katarina." He pushed forward and reached for her hand. "My darling." The endearment, along with compassion in his eyes, cut past her well-laid defenses.

She placed her palm against his.

"Why is this so important to you? Tell me what is driving your resolve. Perhaps I can help."

She trembled at the implication of his words. Did he know what he asked of her? The terrible burden he would take on his shoulders if she answered him truthfully?

Pressing his lips into a grim line, Reiter tugged her against his chest. He held her tightly in his arms, too tightly, as though he feared she would pull away at any moment.

In truth, he had nothing to worry about. She relaxed in his embrace. If only for this one instant, she wanted to rest in this man's strength. He felt real and solid and trustworthy.

"Have faith in me," he whispered into her hair. "Trust me with your secret."

She heard his sincerity. And in that moment, she knew that she could trust him. She *would* trust him. "I have a Jewish ancestor, a maternal grandparent."

Her words were barely audible but she knew he'd heard her because his already tight hold squeezed even more.

She struggled to free herself.

He loosened his embrace and stepped back first. His blue eyes stared at her for a long moment, giving her a glimpse into their unguarded depths. She saw pain. Raw pain.

"Does Schmidt know?"

"*No.* And he can never find out. No one can find out." She grasped his arm. "My mother must not be put in danger."

"I understand."

He took her hand, placed a soft kiss on her palm, and then stepped back again. Although he'd created physical distance, she detected no other withdrawal in him. In fact, with his stiff shoulders and strained gaze, he looked as tortured as she felt.

"Don't look at me that way," she whispered.

He cupped her cheek with his palm, the rough calluses warm against her skin. "You are very brave, Katarina."

She leaned into his hand. "I am no such thing. I… I'm frightened all the time."

"Then why?" He lowered his hand slowly. "Why do you stay in Germany? Why—" He cut off his own words. "Your mother."

"Yes."

He knew everything now.

All the subterfuge between them was gone. There was only honesty left. And truth. The kind of purity of emotion she hadn't known since her childhood.

Unfortunately, she was not a child anymore. She lived in a dangerous world of mean-spirited men with evil agendas. And she'd just laid her secret before a man she'd met only a day ago.

Panic tried to claw to the surface at the realization. Katia shoved the emotion back with a hard swallow. And then she did something she hadn't done since she was nine years old. She prayed.

Heavenly Father, please let this man be worthy of my trust.

What if God still ignored her? What if she'd said the prayer too late?

She knew so little about this man. Nothing, really. Nothing, except the fact that he was a dangerous spy with his own set of personal agendas.

And she'd just admitted the one thing that could get her and her mother killed.

What had she done?

She'd become weak. He'd made her weak with his sincerity and answering pain.

She was vulnerable now, completely at his mercy. If he proved false, who would rescue her? God? The Lord hadn't saved her father. Why would He save her now?

Her hand flew to her throat. She'd made a terrible blunder with her confession. What if—

"No, Katarina. Don't fear me." He pulled her into his arms once again. "I will never hurt you. Never."

She believed him.

Lord, Lord, why bring this man to me now? When there is still so much work to be done in Germany, so many lives to save and so little time left?

Pressed against him, she could feel his heart beating as hard as her own.

"We have much to discuss," Reiter said. "But I cannot put off my...errand any longer."

"Please, take me with you." She couldn't bear to do nothing, not when she'd been the one to compromise the mission.

"It's too dangerous." He released a long breath of air. "Let me take you home. I'll come for you once I've completed my task and we'll talk. Really talk."

The look he gave her was full of promises. He was no longer the jaded spy or hardened skeptic she'd met the night before. He was a man smitten with her, a man she could trust wholeheartedly, a man willing to protect her with his life.

She'd seen a similar look before, in a number of masculine gazes. But this time she knew the same unguarded expression was there in her eyes, as well.

"Trust me, Katarina," he whispered. "I will help you. And your mother."

Her heart softened toward him.

She was lost. Deeply and truly lost.

"All right," she agreed. "You may take me home."

"You'll wait for me there?"

"I'll wait." *For as long as you ask.*

At the yielding look in Katarina's eyes, Jack caught his breath. He wanted to be worthy of such unabashed trust. He had no idea if he was. *Lord, don't let me fail this woman. I need Your strength.*

Would his short prayer be enough? After all the sins he'd committed, would God hear him now when another person's life depended on his actions?

Afraid for them both, Jack lowered his head toward Katarina's and then stopped halfway down.

What was he doing?

He took a step back and shoved a hand through his hair.

Head swimming, muscles tense, he took another step back, away from temptation, away from a woman who had the power to take his mind off his duty. All because she'd had the courage to admit her deadly secret to him.

Katarina Kerensky was the bravest person he knew.

He tried to refocus his thoughts, concentrating his efforts on what must be done to protect her. The first was to complete their mission on his own. Tonight.

The rest they would decide later.

"Once I drop you off at your house, I will return as quickly as possible." He kept his voice just above a whisper. He didn't want to frighten her, but if she had a Jewish relative—no matter how distant—she was in real danger.

And so was her mother, which added layers of unpleasant dimensions to an already precarious situation. At least the silent warnings and contradictions he'd seen in Elena Kerensky's eyes made better sense now.

"Perhaps we should be on our way." She pivoted in the direction of his hotel room.

He saw her hesitate, then visibly take hold of herself. She regretted her confession.

He would not allow her to buckle under fear now.

"No, Katarina, don't let doubt into your heart." He

drew up behind her. "You've trusted me this far, trust me a little while longer."

She turned to face him. "Do you really think this can end well?" A silent plea shimmered in her eyes.

The Lord's words washed over him again. *Never will I leave you; never will I forsake you.* The promise came stronger this time, clearer. As did the sense of peace Jack had thought no longer existed for him.

God had never left him. Jack had been the one to turn away. He'd convinced himself he was alone as Friedrich Reiter. But perhaps atonement began with the simple acknowledgment of the Lord's hand in his life, even in this deadly time of war.

Especially in this deadly time of war.

"Maybe we both need a little more faith," he said aloud.

"Faith?" She angled her head in a show of genuine confusion at his choice of words. "Faith in what? Each other?"

"No. That will take time," he admitted. "What I meant," he said as he took a deep breath, "was faith in God."

He saw the light of optimism in her eyes, right before her face crumbled into a look of stark agony. "God turned His back on me a long time ago."

How many times had Jack thought that same thing in the last two years of his life? Too many times to count. An intense wave of sadness passed through him, sadness for her, for him, for them both. "I understand how you feel, Katarina." He pressed his palm against her cheek again. "More than you know."

Her expression wavered, softened, then firmly closed, as his own would have done had someone said those same words to him before this afternoon. He dropped his hand to his side. "Now is not the time for this discussion."

"No. In that we agree."

Putting his mind back on the mission, he led her into the hotel room then directed her to the open suitcase positioned on the table beside the radio. Opening a hidden panel, he pointed to the cabinet key he'd had made from the wax impression.

She lifted her eyes to his, a question lit in their depths.

"In case something happens to me tonight." He left the rest unspoken.

The quick flash of terror in her eyes—terror for him—caught him by surprise and another layer of his hard exterior melted away.

Katarina Kerensky had done what no other woman had done before. She'd nudged her way into his heart with her convictions and sacrifices and genuine concern for his safety.

Would this brave woman be his salvation, or his ultimate doom?

Chapter Sixteen

21 November 1939, Sengwarden, Wilhelmshaven, 1900 Hours

The promise of a long, hard winter roared into the harbor on a fierce wind off the North Sea. Grim faced and resolute, Admiral Karl Doenitz studied the snow whipping past his office window. The blinding winter wonderland only added depth to his growing headache.

Turning away from the view, Doenitz settled a scowl on the young sailor standing at attention on the other side of his desk. Cold fury tried to work free, but he vowed to listen to the boy's excuses before determining his ultimate fate in the *Kriegsmarine*.

Clasping his hands behind his back, Doenitz got straight to the point. "I understand, *Fähnrich* Heintzman, that you had an unusual meeting last evening." He snapped out the statement with a flick of steel in his voice.

Staring straight ahead, Heintzman's face remained

blank. But Doenitz saw behind the mask. Just past the layer of shock stood fear, surprise and guilt. It was the guilt that interested Doenitz most. "Well?"

"I… Yes, sir, it was quite unusual."

Doenitz picked up Heintzman's report off his desk. He'd already interviewed five of the six guards on duty last evening. Heintzman was the last. "And yet I see you failed to include any mention of the incident in your report."

A muscle in the boy's cheek jerked. "I didn't think it was worth mentioning, sir."

"You didn't think?" In a fit of uncharacteristic rage, Doenitz slammed down the paper on the desk. "It is not your place to think, *Fähnrich,* but to follow procedure."

"I…" Heintzman wisely trailed off and waited for Doenitz to continue.

"When a sailor is given an order, it doesn't matter whether he *thinks* the order serves any purpose." Outrage made Doenitz's voice low and deadly. "He obeys without question."

"I regret not serving my Fatherland to my utmost ability."

Under normal circumstances, Karl Doenitz considered himself a fair man. Although these were anything but normal circumstances, he hesitated from instituting rough justice just yet. "Perhaps it is not too late to save what is left of your career, *Obermaat.*"

Heintzman choked down a loud gulp. *"Obermaat?"*

"The demotion is the least of your worries. Know that

I will issue formal charges if you refuse to cooperate completely from this moment forward."

Heintzman opened his mouth, closed it and then nodded.

Doenitz picked up the report again, skimmed it quickly. Normally, he hated to repeat himself but as he reviewed the incomplete notations, renewed anger clutched around his heart, and he slammed the paper onto the desk a second time. "I want to know the name of this actress, the one you bragged about meeting to your fellow guards but failed to mention in your report."

It was training, or perhaps self-preservation, that had the sailor answering without hesitation. "Katarina Kerensky."

As he let the significance of the boy's revelation sink in, Doenitz came around his desk. "*The* Katarina Kerensky?"

"Yes, sir."

"She is one of the most well-known names in Germany, perhaps in the world. Are you telling me that she came into this obscure fishing village, yet you failed to report the incident?"

"She promised me tickets to her play and a trip backstage if I kept our meeting quiet." His voice shook, as though he'd only just realized how damning his explanation sounded.

"She asked you to keep the incident to yourself?"

"She wasn't alone. She was with a man, they were…" The boy's gaze darted around the room, dropped to the floor, lifted again. "They didn't want stares."

"Katarina Kerensky came here, to Wilhelmshaven of all places, for a tryst?"

"That was my understanding."

It was plausible, Doenitz admitted to himself. A famous woman would certainly want anonymity if she were involved in something so inappropriate. In such a case, leaving the city made perfect sense. Except, of course, that the woman's secret jaunt to Wilhelmshaven was on the exact night as the break-in into the commanding officer's private quarters.

Doenitz thought of the tiny window in his bedroom. The dimensions were far too small for a man to fit through, but perfect for a woman. She would have needed help getting in, however, just as she had needed help—with the use of his chair—to get back out. Hence, the addition of a lover. "You said she was with a man. What was this man's name?"

Heintzman divided a cautious look between Doenitz and the floor, eventually settling on the floor. "I didn't get his name."

"You didn't get it, or he didn't offer it?"

"Both. Neither. I mean—"

"I know what you mean." Doenitz drew himself up. "What did this man look like?"

Heintzman took a deep breath then let it out slowly. "Nordic. Tall, dark blond hair, large frame. Definitely an officer, he had that kind of command about him. But he wasn't in uniform."

"What was he wearing?"

"I don't remember." The seaman's eyebrows slammed together. "It was dark. He blended with the night."

"And he didn't offer his name, or insist you make a report?"

"No, sir. He looked, well, uh, that is, he kissed Fräulein Kerensky like a man in love."

"You saw the two kiss?"

Heintzman gave a clipped affirmative and added, "Under a streetlight."

"They kissed out in the open. But earlier you said they came to Wilhelmshaven to avoid stares."

"Yes, sir, that's what they told me. Which was why they were dressed in black, perhaps?"

"All black? Both of them?"

"Yes. I remember now. I thought it odd at first, until they explained their need for secrecy. Oh, and the fräulein was wearing pants."

Now they were getting somewhere. "Not an evening dress?"

"No, sir."

Another discrepancy. Another step closer to uncovering the identity of the intruder. Every instinct told Doenitz he had found his man. Or rather, *woman*.

But why would Katarina Kerensky break into his private quarters? And who was the man with her? What, exactly, had they been after? Doenitz knew if he found the answer to one question, he would find the answer to the rest.

Ignoring Heintzman for a moment, he advanced to the other end of his desk and rummaged through a stack of personal correspondence. Pulling out a crisp white square of heavy parchment, he studied the invitation's gold-embossed lettering. Elena Kerensky's annual ball hadn't been an event he'd relished attending.

Until now.

Surely the woman's daughter, the famous princess turned stage actress, would be in attendance with all the other important men and women of the Third Reich.

That was it, of course. Instead of waiting for the intruder to come to him a second time, Doenitz would approach him, or rather her, first.

Now that he knew who he was looking for, and where he could find her, time was on his side. He would go to the ball as planned. He would watch. He would assess.

With one small mistake on her part, and cold, clear thinking on his part, the woman would be his in no time.

He simply needed to proceed with patience.

Fortunately, Admiral Karl Doenitz was a *very* patient man.

By the time Jack arrived at Kiel, the cold mist in the air had become a milky-white shroud. The fog all but strangled the meager light from the waxing moon. Testing the depth of visibility, Jack thrust out his hand in front of him. The lower half of his arm disappeared into the thick soup.

He would have to rely on his memory of the shipyard's position and layout from the blueprints he'd studied earlier that morning in Himmler's car.

With slow, cautious steps, Jack approached the complex from the southeast, cloaking himself inside the impenetrable fog. The crack of boot to ground had him freezing in midstep. The noise came again, behind him and off to his left. Loud, precise, unmistakable.

Cocking his head, Jack listened to the cadence of boots hitting gravel. Click, a short pause, another click, pause. Click, pause, click, pause...

One man. Twenty feet away, his footsteps striking the hard, frozen ground in a slow but steady rhythm.

Glad he'd left Kerensky in the safety of her own home, Jack blew into his cupped palms, flexed his fingers, then pulled out his gun. Crouched low, he slipped into the edge of the dense forest, cleared his mind. And waited.

In a matter of seconds, a beam of light arced in a right-to-left pattern on the road.

Jack couldn't make out the exact uniform the guard wore, or the type of rifle he carried. However, he could hear the man muttering to himself, grumbling about the cold weather and the rotten shift he'd pulled three nights in a row.

An amateur. Probably local police.

Jack knew he could avoid detection by letting the guard continue on his way. But if Jack could silence the man now, his exit out of the shipyard would go much smoother.

Decision made, Jack holstered his gun. He wouldn't have to kill the man, just render him temporarily useless.

As the guard passed by, Jack fell into step behind him. He couldn't actually see his quarry, only the sweeping light on the road at his feet.

Jack stepped forward. He could hear the man's

breathing now, *feel* his nervous energy crackling like electricity on the air.

Another step and Jack slipped his left arm around the man's throat, palm over his mouth, and yanked him backward. The flashlight tumbled to the ground, clicked off at the moment of impact.

Using the thumb of his right hand, Jack applied pressure to the guard's wrist until the gun fell onto the gravel with a dull thud.

Flailing hands came up in a wild fight to fend off Jack's attack. Jack tightened his grip, and the hands fell away.

After another moment, the guard started making odd gurgling sounds.

Self-reproach tried to rise inside Jack, guilt tried to blunt his edge and make him quit before he had the man subdued.

Jack turned off his mind, adjusted his hold, let his training take over.

The gurgling sounds morphed into strangled gasps.

Enough was enough.

A quick blow to the temple and the guard went limp.

Silently, Jack laid his prey onto the ground, far enough off the road to avoid detection.

He took an extra moment to check for a pulse at the throat. The beat against his fingertip came slow, steady, but strong enough to tell Jack he'd done no permanent damage to the man.

Working quickly now, Jack emptied the bullets from the guard's gun, stashed them in his pocket, and then tossed the weapon into the dense underbrush lining the road.

Retrieving the flashlight, he flicked the switch. The shaft of light flickered, then died. Jack flung aside the useless object and listened to the movements of the night.

Somewhere in the distance, a foghorn wailed, deep and low. The sound kicked him into action.

Moving slowly, he proceeded forward, pausing every few steps to listen and recalculate his position.

At an estimated fifteen yards from the front gate of the shipyard he crouched low. Blood pounded loudly in his ears, making it hard to hear. He took several deep breaths until his pulse steadied.

For several more minutes, he simply listened to the movement of the guard at the front gate, or rather lack of movement. The rhythmic breathing indicated a deep sleep.

Another amateur.

Rising, Jack trekked silently through the gate no more than two feet from the slumbering guard.

Simplicity was often very effective.

Veering left, Jack took a moment to gather his bearings.

Halos of golden mist surrounded a large pole light, creating a murky beacon in the center of the complex. As he worked his way to the northeast quadrant of the yard, he continued to gauge his surroundings.

A light breeze kicked up, sending damp fog slithering along the concrete walls of the cavernous submarine bays. Three massive cranes loomed over ships in various stages of completion.

Everywhere he looked, giant rubber hoses crisscrossed over one another along the ground, presenting a perilous walkway. Hammers, saws, rivet guns and grinders sat in neat rows along metal shelves to the left of the dry docks.

The Krupp-Germaniawerft looked like every other shipyard. However, considering the nature of the work commissioned by the *Kriegsmarine,* Jack thought it was odd that he found no guards patrolling the inner perimeter of the complex.

A trap? Or typical German arrogance? Were the owners of the shipyard so consumed with keeping intruders out, that they had left themselves vulnerable to attack from the inside?

Jack stayed hidden in the shadows as he made his way to the U-boat pens. He quickly located U-116 by its size and position facing the Bay of Kiel.

A small loading crane lay just to the left of the sub, but there was no cache of weapons waiting to be hauled up.

Were the mines already inside the U-boat?

Prepared to enter the steel beast, Jack crossed to the wooden walkway leading to the deck. But he froze as a beam of light swung next to his feet.

So. There was a roaming guard, after all.

Wheeling around, Jack slipped behind the tall stack of the U-boat. Heart hammering in his chest, he tapped in to the man he'd once been. He closed his eyes and prayed. *Lord, I need Your courage and protection tonight.*

The light swept past again. Left to right. Right to left. Jack counted off the seconds between each arc. By his calculations, the guard was closing in on him.

Running out of time, Jack considered his options.

He could scramble into the U-boat, but the beam of light was getting closer. Too close. As much as he hated failure, Jack couldn't risk capture now that he was this far into the mission.

He would simply have to wait for the guard to complete his sweep of the complex before climbing into the U-boat.

Resigned, Jack settled into position to wait.

And then the shouting began.

Chapter Seventeen

Jack froze as the individual shouts blended into one long, angry spurt of German.

All at once, several floodlights burst to life, creating a muted halo of light around each pole. The crack and buzz of electricity surging through ice-coated wires overwhelmed the other noises.

But soon the angry shouts prevailed once more.

Crouching low, Jack stayed in position behind the U-boat stack. In spite of the cold air, he started sweating. He considered ducking inside the sub, but the odds of getting out undetected were heavily against him. The U-boat could easily become his coffin.

He opted to wait it out a bit longer.

One voice lifted above the others, and Jack was finally able to make out the individual words.

He didn't like what he heard.

The guard he had hit on the head had recovered. As a result, every man on duty was searching for the intruder.

His primary goal now was to get out of the shipyard as quickly and as quietly as possible.

He began to walk briskly toward the outer rim of the yard, away from the commotion. He had to fight the need to rush his steps. Catching sight of three pale beams of light vibrating through the fog, he changed direction.

Never will I leave you; never will I forsake you.

Fusing with the shadows, Jack clung to God's promise as he moved at an angle perpendicular to the one he'd used to enter the yard.

Lord, be with me now. I can't succeed without Your help.

After a few more steps, he stopped again, listened to the raised voices and scrambling of feet. He guessed five, maybe six men.

Using the fog to blanket his movements, Jack crept to his left, dropped under a beam that swept just over his head.

He rose again. Took three more steps. Dropped under the next beam of light. He repeated the procedure again and again and again, until the last guard had moved to the back of the yard and Jack had moved closer to the front.

Taking slow, even breaths, Jack let his mind work through the alternatives. He knew once they'd searched the immediate grounds, the guards would fan out, covering one mile at a time. As bad as he wanted to study a mine up close, Jack couldn't stay in the area any longer.

His only chance to avoid capture was to get to his

car and out of Kiel before the search expanded past the main perimeter of the shipyard.

As he melted into the mist, he could hear the clumsy guards shouting at one another.

Using the voices to pinpoint each man's position, Jack moved in a wide, cautious circle along the outer rim of the chaos. Keeping his eyes and ears open, he quickly slipped free of the yard.

He took a single step, and then his foot slipped. The resulting crunch of gravel was unmistakable.

Jack flung himself into a run.

They hadn't seen him yet, but it wouldn't be long now.

The rapid report of gunfire trailed in his wake. He picked up speed. A bullet whizzed by his head and drove harmlessly into the underbrush.

Another bullet hurled past him. And another. Jack heard a muffled pop, felt a burning sting high on his left arm.

He'd been hit, but he didn't slacken his pace.

Allowing adrenaline to fuel his steps, he continued in the direction of his car. After several minutes of running flat out, the shouts became distant murmurs. His own labored breathing filled his ears, distracting him, but Jack forced his mind to focus, to numb all other thoughts except one—*escape*.

He entered the edge of the forest. Diving into the thick foliage, he pitched around the front of his car, fumbled with the lock.

Throwing the gearshift into Neutral, he wheeled the

car silently back onto the road, letting out a gush of air at the pain in his left arm.

With mechanical movements, he slipped behind the wheel, fired the engine and steered the car south toward Hamburg. He checked the mirrors, relieved that no one followed him. *Yet.*

Not taking any chances, he pressed the accelerator hard against the floorboard.

With one whiff, he caught the scent of his own blood. He took his eyes off the road for a split second and looked at his left arm. He was bleeding badly. Unfortunately, he would have to wait until he had more distance between him and Kiel to tend to the wound.

Lord, God, please protect me a little while longer.

A sense of peace fell over him. Breathing slower now, he took stock of the situation.

He was alive. He'd avoided capture. But he hadn't been able to study an actual mine. He'd also left a witness, alive and talking. Worst of all, he'd been shot.

He tentatively flexed his left bicep, gave a grunt at the burst of pain.

"Lord," Jack prayed out loud as darkness crept along the edges of his vision, "if this is the end of my life, will You welcome me home, or are my sins too great?"

Part of his mother's favorite verse came to mind. *While we were still sinners, Christ died for us…*

"Is that promise for me, too, Lord? My sins are more than most."

But God demonstrates His own love for us in this: While we were still sinners, Christ died for us… Jack heard the words clearly in his mind. In response, God's peace that transcended all understanding flowed through every fiber of his body.

But then the wind picked up, sending one vicious gust after another in a sideswiping pattern against the car. He focused once more on his driving. The effort to ignore the aching in one arm and control the car with the other stole his breath away.

By the time he felt safe enough to pull off the road, Jack had to lean his head against the steering wheel and gulp for air.

He tried to swallow between breaths, but his mouth was dry as dust. A bad sign, indicating he'd lost a considerable amount of blood.

First things first. He needed to stop the bleeding, before he passed out from the pain and loss of blood.

Setting the brake, he pushed away from the steering wheel, shifting until he had enough room to work unhindered.

He tugged aside his sweater, yanked his shirt free, and then ripped off a strip along the bottom seam. Working as quickly as he could with only one good hand, he rolled the material into a makeshift tourniquet. He then tied off the flow of blood to the wound with a pull of his teeth on one end and his free hand on the other.

His efforts were clumsy and inefficient, but he knew the bandage would hold until he made it back to Katia's house.

He pulled his shirt closed, shrugged into the jacket he'd left on the seat then checked his watch. He tried to calm his mind, but no matter how slowly he breathed, he couldn't seem to focus.

Dragging a hand down his face, he fought to keep his mind free of worry. *Fear not:* the most often stated command in the Bible. Worry was nothing more than the absence of faith.

Faith. Yes, he was slowly realizing he still had a little faith left—though he'd surrendered much to the war effort—far too much.

From this point forward, he would manage what he could manage, and surrender the rest to God.

I am in Your hands, Lord. Your power is made perfect in my weakness.

Favoring his left arm, Jack steered the car back onto the road and pressed down on the accelerator.

In spite of his failure at the shipyard, he still had to keep his appointment with Himmler at 2300 hours. He would be ready. Too many innocent lives were at stake to go into the meeting unprepared, including the lives of a certain Russian stage actress and her blue-blooded mother.

Jack frowned at the road ahead.

Katarina Kerensky's involvement in this mission had been problematic from the start. Considering the secret she'd revealed to him earlier, Jack could no longer endanger her life. By rescuing her, perhaps he could begin the process of becoming an agent of protection rather than an agent of death.

His vision blurred again. Oblivion beckoned. But Jack set his jaw at a hard angle. This mission was far from over. He still had much work to do this night.

First order of business: send Katarina Kerensky packing for the next flight out of Germany.

* * *

By the time Jack arrived at Katarina's, the pain in his left arm had become a burning throb. His vision blurred, again. How many times was that? He'd lost count after four. He blinked—hard. The smudge of gray in the center of his eyes didn't go away.

His ears started ringing, but he managed to stagger to the bottom of her front steps without incident. There was no outdoor lighting so he could at least stumble along in obscurity. Thankfully, he'd memorized the yard's layout the last time he was here.

Before navigating the first step he took a moment to catch his breath. He was no stranger to pain. He'd been shot other times. However, he *was* human. And he knew his body well enough to know that two important limbs, primarily the ones holding him upright, were about to give out on him.

He needed to get his arm bandaged, deal with his dehydration then be on his way. He could not miss his meeting with Himmler. There was the important matter of damage control now.

Sending up a prayer for strength, he tripped up four of the five steps. He lost his balance, righted himself just as quickly. All he had to do was climb that last one—which seemed to be getting farther away with every blink. Once inside Katarina's house, he would take a moment to clear his head. That's what he would do first. After he had his equilibrium back he would tell her the whole story of his failed trip to Kiel. She deserved the full truth. She...

Lord, I'm tired.

In a final burst of energy, Jack shoved up the final

step. And collapsed against the door. He closed his eyes and waited. One more burst of energy. He needed a little help here. No, he needed a lot of help.

He called on an old staple.

The Lord is my shepherd, he prayed, *I shall not want. He maketh me to lie down in green pastures: He leadeth me beside the still waters...*

Perhaps Jack would stay here awhile. Praying felt that good.

Now where was he?

Yea, though I walk through the valley of the shadow of death, I will fear no evil: for Thou art with me...

He couldn't stay here much longer and risk discovery by the wrong person.

Thou preparest a table before me in the presence of mine enemies...

Another moment of rest, he promised himself, just one more moment and he would pull together his strength and knock.

I will dwell in the house of the Lord for ever!

Just one...more...moment...of rest...

Chapter Eighteen

Katia woke with a start.

Disoriented, she pushed to a sitting position and then rubbed the sleep out of her eyes. She couldn't remember what had startled her. Or why she was on the couch in her living room.

She'd been exhausted when Reiter had dropped her off, mentally and physically worn out from the events of the last two days. That much she remembered. But she wasn't usually so slow to regain her focus.

The room had grown dark, with only a few shadows dancing across the wall in front of her.

Still trying to pull her thoughts together, she shifted her gaze to the clock on the far wall—9:00 p.m., 2100 hours.

Her mind cleared at once. Where was Friedrich? He'd said he wouldn't be long. Why wasn't he back yet?

A maelstrom of emotions had her flattening her hand against her stomach. Familiar panic rose up. Only a matter of hours ago, she'd confessed her darkest secret to a man she'd known less than two days.

Would he prove trustworthy?

Yes. Yes, he would. She couldn't put her reasons into words, but she knew he was the only man she could trust, the first since her father had died.

But why him? Was it because he'd mentioned God with such conviction in his eyes, as though he'd rediscovered his own faith and wanted her to have that same hope?

Even as she pondered such a miracle, a nagging premonition had her shoving her hair off her face.

Something wasn't right.

She tipped her head and listened past the silence in the room. A sound was coming from her front door.

Knocking? No. More like scratching.

She gave herself a little push and stood. Her legs wobbled underneath her. Obviously, she needed more sleep. She didn't have the luxury.

The scratching came again, more insistent this time.

Was it her mother and Hermann, come to get her for a late supper? She'd claimed a headache earlier and had told them she wouldn't be available for the rest of evening. Surely, they would respect her wishes and take her at her word.

Padding across the thick carpet, she tried to gather her various roles around her. Which one would she need tonight?

Unsure what to expect, her skin went cold with dread.

Katia swung open the door.

"Friedrich." She was only dimly aware she'd gasped

his name. But he didn't look right. He was swaying. That much she could discern. But his face was curtained in shadows so she couldn't see his eyes.

He stumbled past her, weaving across the entryway of her home. Two more bobbing steps and he reached out to steady himself against the wall on his left.

"Friedrich, what's happened?"

He mumbled an incoherent response in a language that definitely was not German, and in an accent she'd heard only in the movies.

Why would he break cover so noticeably?

Fearing something had gone dreadfully wrong, Katia shut the door behind him and then flicked on the overhead light in the foyer.

Hissing, he covered his eyes against light. "Have mercy, woman." He growled out his words in slurred German.

What was wrong with him?

She pulled his hand down and stared hard at his scowling face. His pupils were dilated and unfocused. "Are you drunk?"

His scowl deepened. "Of course not."

Katia had her doubts, especially when he kept listing to his left. She took a sniff of the air around him and reared back. He didn't smell of liquor. He smelled of... *blood*.

A thousand questions shot to her lips but something dark and wet on his left sleeve caught her attention. "You're bleeding."

She had no appropriate role for this unexpected development.

He looked down at his arm. His eyes widened, as though he was surprised to find his sleeve coated with his own blood. "Looks like the tourniquet didn't hold."

"Is that all you have to say?" Her concern made her words sound sharper than she'd intended.

"It's just a scratch." He waved his hand with a dismissive flick. The gesture threw him off balance again.

She reached out to steady him, he tripped back a step and she missed.

"You need to sit down," she said.

"I'm fine." He rocked back on his heels and then threw himself forward. "Nothing to worry about."

"I see that."

"Let me take care of this first." He clawed at the bloody tourniquet on his arm. "Then we'll talk before I go to my meeting with Himmler."

"Himmler? Heinrich Himmler? You have a meeting with the head of the SS? Tonight?" Just how deep undercover was this man?

"Don't worry, Katarina." He placed his good hand on her shoulder. "You haven't been compromised. Everything will be fine."

Fine? He used that word rather loosely. Nothing would be fine as long as men like Adolf Hitler and Heinrich Himmler were in power. Nothing would be fine as long as dissenters were silenced and people like Katia's mother were openly targeted for their Jewish heritage.

"Now. If you could direct me to your washroom."

Still in a state of shock, she automatically pointed over his shoulder.

He turned and swiftly lost his footing.

She caught him by the right elbow. "I'll come with you."

He didn't argue. Instead, he looked grateful, and a little lost, as though he wasn't used to being the one in need and didn't know what to do with the change in their roles.

She wasn't altogether sure herself.

Once in the bathroom, she filled a glass with water and handed it to him. "Here. You look like you could use this."

With a trembling hand, he brought the cup to his lips and gulped the entire contents in one taking. A little less shaky now, he filled the glass again and brought it to his mouth a second time.

She stopped him before he could drink. "No. Slow down. Too much will make you sick."

"I…" He looked at her in cautious silence then set the cup on the counter. "You're right."

"Take off your jacket and let me look at your wound." She spoke calmly, but her heart beat hard against her ribs. What had happened tonight? Where had he gone?

He must have read a portion of her thoughts because she saw the flash of some deep emotion in his eyes— apology, guilt, pain? She shook her head as she turned to the sink and ran warm water over a washcloth.

"It really is just a scratch," he mumbled. "The bullet missed its mark."

"Thank You, Lord," she whispered. It wasn't much of a prayer, but she was a bit out of practice these days.

Taking a deep breath, she left the washcloth in the

sink and turned to face him again. "All right, let's have a look."

Grimacing, he shrugged out of his jacket then pulled off the useless tourniquet. Clearly exhausted from the effort, he sank onto the only seat available in the room. "There. I'm all yours."

Ignoring the little jolt of pleasure at his absolute surrender, Katia glanced down at his arm. From elbow to wrist his sleeve was coated with a thick layer of blood. She wanted to sob. And then throw up. But she was too afraid to give in to either impulse right now. Later, she promised herself, when she was alone, she would give in to the sickness. And then maybe the fear.

For now, she had to concentrate.

This man's life was in her hands, the same hands she couldn't keep from shaking. She had no practice for this, no protective barrier to put in front of the real Katia. She cared for him that much, this man who had dug past all her layers of defense. A dark uneasiness crept over her at the thought.

She must have stood there, unmoving, for quite a while, because he went to work on his arm all by himself.

Stone-faced, he ripped apart the sleeve at the shoulder and then peeled the soaked material away from the wound, inch by brutal inch. He made no sound, nor did he wince, but his eyes glazed over with each passing second.

Katia wanted to weep for him. He had such strength, such courage. He would be an easy man to love.

She shut her eyes a moment, shuddered and then

swallowed the last of her hesitation. With her fingers still trembling, she took over. Moving his hand out of the way, she wiped at the blood on his arm with the warm, soapy cloth from the sink.

"I can do it myself," he offered, as if he knew how hard this was for her.

A deep affection surged through her. Even in the midst of his own agony, he thought of her first. She felt exposed under such raw concern.

What was she going to do now?

"Right." She gave her words a hard edge to hide her confusion. "Your previous efforts were very efficient."

He smiled a little, a very little. "I made it here in one piece, didn't I?"

"If you say so."

"I say so."

What if he hadn't made it back to her alive? What if the bullet *had* hit its mark? The thought was too awful to contemplate so she cleared her mind and focused only on what she could control—taking care of his wound.

She placed the cloth under the running faucet and rinsed out the blood. So much blood, she thought. Too much.

She slid a quick look at him from under her lashes and felt her stomach flip inside itself. Even with his skin pale and his mouth tight from gritting past the pain, he mesmerized her. It wasn't his masculine beauty alone that got to her. It was his inner strength. She recognized a man of integrity when she saw one.

How would she ever survive knowing such a man?

Sighing, she wrung out the cloth one last time and went back to work.

Chapter Nineteen

Jack shut his eyes the moment the warm cloth touched his skin again. He nearly whimpered from the effort of holding back a sigh of relief. Katarina's touch was so gentle, her eyes filled with such caring that he felt the sharp stab of some foreign emotion rising up inside him.

Sliding a covert glance at her, he found himself struck all over again by her beauty. He closed his eyes to ward off another rush of unexpected emotions, but her scent filled him. She smelled very female, a combination of zesty white flowers and spice.

Perhaps it was safer to keep his eyes opened.

He wondered where the questions were. She must have at least a few. Didn't women always ask questions? "Don't you want to know how this happened?"

Her brows scrunched in consternation. "Oh, I have a good idea."

With unnecessary force, she tossed the bloody rag into the sink, then quickly pressed a clean, dry cloth to the wound. "You messed up, made a mistake or," she amended as she smiled at him with a look meant to subdue his male arrogance, "probably both."

Jack leveled a gaze that had been known to shrink the toughest of men. "You'll have to work on your gloating, Katarina. It needs a little more hypocrisy in it."

"Is that so?" Her brows lifted slightly. "Then tell me this, am I wrong?"

He broke eye contact. "You're enjoying my failure far too much. It's unbecoming in a woman of your fine breeding, a woman who's had her own share of mistakes during this mission."

"Let's review, shall we?" She pressed the cloth against his wound with a little more efficiency than before. He preferred her more tentative. It hurt less.

Her lips pulled into a frown. "You went somewhere dangerous tonight, alone, without telling me where. And while you were out, doing who knows what, you got yourself shot." The anger was there in her voice, throbbing just below the surface.

"It's not my first bullet wound," he said in his own defense.

"Of course it isn't. You're a man, aren't you?"

"What's that supposed to mean?"

"Hold this steady." She cocked her head at the cloth on his arm.

He did as she requested, flinching when her fingers brushed against his.

Muttering in Russian about foolhardy men who carried guns, she rooted in the cabinet above his head.

He wished she wasn't quite so angry. It was only going to get worse when he told her what happened. For now, he decided to change the subject. "You'll need to work quickly. I have that…meeting I mentioned."

Without looking at him, she pulled out a brown bottle, scissors, bandages and white medical tape. Hands full, she stepped back and then deposited the lot on the counter.

"Right. You want me to patch you up, just like that, and then send you into a meeting with one of the most dangerous men in Germany. Getting shot is that common for you, is it?"

Although he bristled at her words, something in her expression had him wanting to placate her rather than antagonize. "It's just a scratch, Katarina. A scratch."

Her lips pressed into a hard line. "Put there by a bullet meant to take your life." A shudder passed through her.

"Katarina, I—"

"Here comes the fun part." Looking entirely too cheerful, she swabbed another washcloth with what looked—and smelled—suspiciously like iodine.

"No, you don't." Jack shot up then collapsed back down as a jolt of nausea swept through him. After several deep breaths, he cleared the pain out of his mind. But the effort drew a thick sheen of sweat onto his brow. "That stuff stings," he complained once he had his breath again.

"Of course it does. That's how you know it's doing the job." She smiled, sweetly, then pressed the cloth against his wound.

He bit back a howl of pain. The woman had a mean streak. Pure and simple.

Focus. That's what he needed. Focus. His mind was stronger than his body. It was all a matter of concentration, a matter of single-mindedness.

She applied a second coat of iodine.

"Have you no compassion?" he hissed.

"Of course. When it's warranted."

"You're doing this to punish me. You're angry. You're scared. And this is your way of getting back at me."

"I'm doing this to clean your wound. Your *bullet* wound. But, yes." She sighed. "I am angry. Scared, too. Mostly scared."

Before he could respond she pressed her lips to his forehead. "You're going to be fine, Friedrich Reiter. Just fine."

He wanted to relax inside all that tenderness, just for a moment, but he didn't know how. He'd been on his own too long.

He was only just beginning to realize how alone he'd been.

"Yes, Katarina." He touched her hand. "I will be fine. I always am."

Her hands started shaking again. "You could have died tonight."

"But I didn't. I won't—*I can't*—allow fear of death to keep me from doing what needs to get done."

Very carefully, very slowly, she set the bottle and rag on the counter. "People who don't fear death are nothing but reckless. They take foolish risks."

"Do I strike you as either reckless or foolish?"

Her answer was immediate. "No. But—"

"Worry is useless, Katarina. It's also a clear sign that

our faith isn't strong enough. One thing I've learned these last two years, no, these last two *days,* is that it's important to listen to God's voice and guidance, not our own fear and personal agendas."

Like his own personal agenda for revenge. Vengeance was not his. It was God's alone. Jack could no longer in good conscience act without discerning his own motives first. He must be more obedient. He must—

Katarina's sigh broke through his thoughts. "Faith is hard to come by in times such as these."

Who was he to argue? "You're right. Fear, anger and bitterness are always easier. We live in a fallen world. Maybe the question isn't 'why do bad things happen,' rather '*who's* in control when bad things happen.' God will always be bigger than any circumstance."

Her brows squeezed together, but she didn't respond right away. "It's hard not to ask why."

He had no argument to that. "I know."

She let out a shuddering breath. No longer meeting his gaze, she concentrated on wrapping the bandage around his arm and then securing the end with medical tape. "There." She stepped back and eyed her work. "That should do for now."

He rose, took her hand in his.

She tried to turn away. He pulled her closer.

"Thank you, Katarina. Thank you for taking care of my arm." He lifted her chin with his fingertip. "Thank you for taking care of *me.*"

She took a shaky breath, but then visibly relaxed. Reaching up, she touched his cheek. "The next time you decide to strike out on your own, don't. Whether you like it or not, you need me."

A strange calm settled over him. "You're right. I do need you." He wasn't talking solely about the mission.

She, apparently, thought he was. "Where did you go tonight?"

Knowing he owed her the truth, he sat back down. "I went to a shipyard in Kiel. To investigate a U-boat, what I believe is the lead submarine in the magnetic mines mission. I was interrupted before I could finish the job, hence the need for a bandage."

"But." She angled her head at him. "How did you know the U-boat was there and that it was the right one?"

He worked to keep from clenching his jaw. "Himmler told me."

Her eyes widened, but she didn't speak.

"I work...as one of his handpicked agents."

Her hand flew to her throat. "Oh."

He understood her shock. "Rest assured, my loyalties lie with the British. But I also have certain responsibilities to Himmler and his SS."

He expected her to pale at his admission, to show disgust and disbelief, perhaps even terror. But she surprised him. "What a terrible, lonely way to live." Her voice filled with tenderness. "You never know who to trust, do you?"

"I trust you. And I trust God." He spoke the truth from his heart.

Lord, forgive me for relying only on myself. Help me to rely on You more.

With a look of understanding in her eyes, she reached down and touched his face. "Oh, Friedrich."

He stood. Just as he pulled her close she wrapped her arms around his waist and rested her cheek against his chest.

"You are... I don't know how... I wish..." Her words trailed off on a shuddering sigh.

He thought he understood her inability to put her feelings into words. She'd given him the one weapon that could destroy her—information about her heritage— while he'd given her nothing. Not really. Both the British and the Germans knew he worked with the opposing government. He was a traitor one day, a hero the next. It all depended on what day it was and who was sitting on the other side of the desk.

For once, he wanted to share his truth with someone who would look past the spy.

"My name is Jonathon Phillip Anderson," he said in German, but then switched to English to make his point. "I go by Jack, not Jonathon. I'm an American naval engineer on loan to the British from the Office of Naval Intelligence, ONI. I was born in Lincoln, Nebraska, but grew up in Washington, D.C."

With that last bit of information, he'd given her an equally powerful weapon to use against him.

She lifted her head. The awe and respect he saw in her nearly slaughtered him. He wasn't worthy of this courageous woman's loyalty. But he wanted to be.

"That's it, then." She nodded in acknowledgment. "No turning back for either of us. We're in this together, bound by our individual secrets."

"Yes." He thought of the verse from Ecclesiastes. "'Two are better than one,'" he quoted.

She took a deep breath and finished the rest of the verse. "And if one falls the other will pick him—or her—up."

"Precisely." He pulled her close again. He wanted to stay right where he was, holding her tightly to him. Something powerful had just happened between them, a fragile bond that needed nurturing. Unfortunately, they didn't have the liberty to explore their newfound connection. Not tonight.

"I have to meet Himmler in little more than an hour."

"Will he…" She looked up at him. "Are you in danger because you failed tonight?"

He wouldn't lie to her, not now. "I don't know. I have enough information to share that should satisfy him. But no matter what, the SS will not find out about you or your secret. Not from me."

"I know." She lifted her chin. "I trust you completely."

He knew how hard that came for her. In the face of her courage he fell a little in love with her. Maybe more than a little. "Will you do something with me, before I go?"

"Anything."

"I want us to pray, together."

"I… Yes." She gave him a wobbly smile. "I…I think I would like that, too."

He took her hands in his and then knelt on the tile floor at her feet.

After a moment of hesitation, she joined him on the floor.

His arm might still be throbbing. His head might still feel light. Yet with Katarina's hands in his, both of them kneeling before God in total surrender, Jack felt stronger than he had in years.

He closed his eyes.

"Lord, Heavenly Father, we know You are not the author of destruction, but of peace. I pray You guide us in our quest to stop tyranny, tonight and every night to come. Whether we're together or apart." He paused a moment, then recalled a long-forgotten verse from Zechariah. "We will not succeed in our own strength, but by Your spirit alone. In Jesus's name, Amen."

"Amen." Katarina's hands tightened around his.

And with that simple gesture from her, the night turned a whole lot brighter.

Chapter Twenty

21 November 1939, Abwehr headquarters annex,
North Hamburg, 2300 hours

Although it was seconds before 2300 hours, Jack didn't rush his steps. He strode purposely up the front walkway of the rambling three-story mansion. It was an imposing structure, nestled on a knuckle of land perched along craggy cliffs.

The house had been confiscated—most likely from a Jewish family—and turned into the heart of Germany's wireless receiving operation. But this was an *Abwehr* facility, used solely by the military intelligence agency. There was no direct connection to the SS here.

Why had Himmler moved their meeting to this house, of all places, instead of keeping it at the Gestapo headquarters as originally planned?

With the question weighing heavily on his mind, Jack entered the building at precisely 2300 hours. An SS corporal rose from a chair situated in the shadows of the main hall and saluted. "*Heil* Hitler."

"*Heil* Hitler."

"The *Reichsführer* is waiting for you, Herr *Sturmban-nführer*. Please follow me." With a click of his heels, the corporal turned sharply around and led the way down a long corridor.

Jack followed the man along the darkened hallway, through another corridor and then another. As he memorized the route with one part of his brain, he wondered again why Himmler had brought him here of all places.

Was it a test? An intimidation tactic? A reminder that he was being watched closely?

I will never leave you, nor forsake you.

Jack tucked God's promise into his heart, gathering courage from it as he did. Worry was useless. Himmler would reveal his hand when it suited him. And not before.

In the meantime, Jack would do everything in his power to protect Katarina. No harm would come to her because of him. The most effective tool in his arsenal was the coldhearted shell of Friedrich Reiter.

After yet another turn down another twisting corridor, the corporal ushered Jack into a small room furnished with only a dilapidated desk and two wooden chairs. The air smelled sour, heavy, like a moldy bunker.

Another tactic, designed to throw a man off his guard. Friedrich Reiter was not so easily manipulated.

"Herr Himmler will be with you shortly," the corporal said, then retreated.

Once he was alone, Jack remained standing, shoulders back, head high. He lifted his left arm slightly but did not wince at the resulting pain the small gesture caused. Katarina had cleaned the wound and dressed it properly. But he needed rest in order for his body to complete the healing process.

He would take the time after the war.

Turning at the sound of the door creaking on its hinges, he presented a stiff-armed salute as Himmler entered the room. "Herr *Reichsführer*," he said. "*Heil* Hitler."

"*Heil* Hitler."

Jack remained at attention, and waited.

Himmler's restless gaze took in the room, then shifted to Jack's face. "Have a seat, Herr Reiter."

As Jack settled into the less appealing of the two chairs, he noted that Himmler was wearing the black uniform of the Gestapo, the Death's Head prominently displayed above the bill of his cap. The uniform sent a bloody warning. And Jack knew it was no empty threat. Himmler was capable of terrible evil.

I will never leave you, nor forsake you. He relaxed in the reminder of God's truth, and then set aside Jack Anderson for the remainder of the meeting.

"You surprise me, Herr Reiter." Himmler's eyes turned colder, and his voice iced over. "I expected you much later."

"This was our agreed time."

"So it was." He made a grand show of taking off his hat and settling into the other chair. "I understand you took your actress home early this evening, before you had to travel to Kiel."

The statement was meant to let Jack know that Himmler had been monitoring him, personally, along with the Gestapo and various other Nazi agencies.

Friedrich Reiter was a popular man.

"I wanted no distractions from my duties to the Fatherland. I will join her once I leave here. We prefer our privacy, you understand." He punctuated his statement with Reiter's sly smile. It was important Himmler got all the wrong ideas, with one exception. The head of the SS needed to know that Jack was fully aware of the listening devices planted in his hotel room.

"So you are continuing your relationship with the woman."

Jack lifted a careless shoulder. "She has her uses. Aside from the obvious, Admiral Doenitz will be attending her mother's ball tomorrow evening. It's long past time I met the admiral in person."

"You always go beyond the call of duty, Herr Reiter," Himmler said with satisfaction in his tone. "Now, for our other matter. You have news for me?"

Pleased Himmler had changed the direction of the conversation on his own, Jack nodded. Although a certain amount of sharing information was expected, he needed to handle the question of the magnetic mines carefully.

With the cold directness that was Reiter's trademark, Jack leaned forward and lowered his voice. "It is delicate information, Herr *Reichsführer*."

Himmler waved his hand. "It is safe to speak freely here. You may proceed without concern."

"As you wish."

Jack sat back, seemingly relaxed, but he chose to stick to the cautious approach as was in character with his alter ego. He'd failed to investigate U-116 properly, but the head of the SS didn't need to know that. The altercation with the guard was of little importance, as well. Heinrich Himmler cared only about the results of a mission as they pertained to him. He cared nothing of Reiter's methods in retrieving the information.

"The weapon we discussed earlier is a magnetic mine designed especially for submarine use." Jack delivered the information without a single qualm, knowing he'd revealed enough to pit Himmler against Doenitz even more than before. "Its explosive charge carries twice the firepower of traditional torpedoes."

Himmler's eyes gleamed with interest. "Did you say *magnetic* mine?"

"Yes. The U-boats lay a succession of these mines on the bottom of the shallow seabed, mainly near ports and military bases along the British coast. The bombs target ships as they pass by."

Digesting the information, Himmler nodded. "Go on."

"The mines are not discriminating," Jack continued. "Military or merchant, British or American, the target is the closest ship in range."

Himmler's lips thinned. "Then what keeps the mines from blowing up the U-boat once they are released?"

Jack didn't know, hence the problem with designing

his countermeasures for the British. But he had a theory, one he could use to keep Himmler satisfied without jeopardizing Britain's attempts to stop the destruction. "There is a delayed-action trigger, a time fuse of sorts, which does not activate until the U-boat has cleared the area."

Jack stopped his explanation there, counting on Himmler's mind-set as a former chicken farmer to neither understand the complicated science of the bombs, nor wish to try. How the trigger worked was still the unknown factor. And after tonight's failure, Jack was no closer to finding out. He still might have to return to Wilhelmshaven, and Admiral Doenitz's private quarters.

He would do so without Katarina.

Clearly unaware of Jack's thoughts, Himmler drummed his fingers on his thigh. "From what you've told me, it is obvious Doenitz wishes to use the mines to further increase public sentiment for his U-boats. A noble end, to be sure, but the secrecy must end."

Jack bit back a sigh of relief. Himmler was satisfied, even though Jack had given him very little information. In fact, Admiral Doenitz should have shared all of this with the SS long before now.

Internal rivalry within the German state wasn't Jack's concern. Himmler would deal with the admiral's secret-keeping himself. Let the dogs battle one another for a while, that was Jack's philosophy.

Himmler shifted, his blue eyes almost colorless now, nothing more than a slit of drab gray against the black pupils. "You have given me plenty to work with. The Führer will be pleased."

Jack nodded, then answered with his well-rehearsed line. "It is my honor to be of service to my Führer, and the Fatherland."

"Very good. Now." Rising, Himmler crossed to a small window, and stared out into the black night for several long seconds.

"I have another opportunity for you," he said, spinning back to face Jack. "It would enable you to return to the Fatherland, perhaps permanently. And it would take advantage of the skills you've acquired in the last two years."

Jack sat perfectly still, waiting, swallowing back a mixture of trepidation and excitement. This was it, then. All roads had led to this moment. He had pushed to get himself here, to the one assignment that would take him deep inside the SS.

"I only wish to serve," he said. But not the Fatherland.

In that moment, Jack put his hope in God and surrendered completely to the Lord's will for his life. He would no longer seek revenge for his own purpose. He would have confidence in the Lord's ability to use him as an instrument to defeat the Nazis' evil.

"What I have in mind would utilize your unique skills," Himmler said again. "That is, if you are interested."

Jack leaned forward. By nature, he was a patient man, but he could feel his heart pounding with anticipation. Or was it fear? He wanted to hear what Himmler had in mind, wanted to see if all the sacrifices of the last two years were about to pay off.

Even if the outcome meant Jack would have to lay

down his own life, the price would be worth it if he could save innocent blood. This was no longer about Jack. It was about courageous people like Katarina Kerensky. It was about a higher plan and service to God.

"I'm interested," he said.

"As you know, I do not trust Admiral Canaris any more than I trust Admiral Doenitz."

Keeping his expression blank, Jack nodded. The lack of trust between Himmler and the head of the *Abwehr* was no secret. The fact that they were having this conversation in an *Abwehr* facility revealed Himmler's serpentine mind and deadly arrogance. The choice of meeting places made perfect sense now. The mouse was actually plotting against the cat inside the cat's own den.

"What is it you want me to do?" Jack asked, certain he'd come to the most important moment of his thirty-two years.

Every small, seemingly inconsequential life decision had prepared him to take on this task. He'd memorized countless Scriptures as a boy, which would now become his primary source of God's Word while ensconced in the heart of the Nazi regime. He'd trained as an engineer and joined the Navy at precisely the right time to warrant the German's interest in him.

Perhaps even losing his way for a time had brought him to a deeper conviction to serve the Lord.

"We will put you in a position within the *Abwehr* itself. You will report back to me any suspicious dealings between Canaris and his closest agents." The smile he sent Jack was as hard and cold as an artic blast.

"Admiral Canaris will allow this?"

Himmler released a vicious chuckle. "He has no choice." That arrogant statement proved the unconscionable power Himmler had acquired within the Third Reich. Even men of equal standing now had to fear the head of the SS.

Proceed carefully, Jack. You are dealing with a madman.

"What of my work inside England?" he asked. It was a reasonable question. An expected one. "I've built a solid cover over the last two years."

"At all costs, you will not jeopardize your situation with the Americans, or MI6. I may need you to return to one or both countries in the future."

A ball of dread rolled ice-hot in his belly. Could Jack do this? No, he couldn't. Not on his own. But he could with God's strength. *I can do all things through Christ who strengthens me.*

"I understand, Herr *Reichsführer*. I will not let you down."

"Tie up any loose ends as quickly as possible. I want you in Berlin within the month."

Within the month. Jack had thirty days to get Katarina and her mother out of Germany.

And then he would be completely entrenched inside the identity of Friedrich Reiter. For a moment, all his guilt and rage rose to the surface.

Jack shoved the emotions back down with a hard swallow. He was a changed man, thanks to meeting Katarina. Her courage had inspired him to return to the God-fearing man he'd been before Reiter had attacked him.

This world was filled with wickedness, but Jack would no longer allow his anger over what the Nazis had done to him to block his confidence in God's ability to defeat evil. He would call on God alone for his strength now.

After two long years of preparation, he would have his chance to become an instrument for good. In thirty days he would infiltrate the internal security service of the SS—the *Sicherheitsdienst,* or SD.

This was it. The moment he'd planned for since Friedrich Reiter had come to take his life. Jack was ready.

Chapter Twenty-One

22 November 1939, Sengwarden, Wilhelmshaven
Kriegsmarine headquarters, 0700 hours

Admiral Doenitz spread the set of blueprints across the top of his desk, for the moment ignoring the U-boat captain standing at attention beside him. He took his time studying the drawings. The revolutionary mines were the most powerful naval weapons ever designed. But the bombs would only be effective if they remained secret.

Satisfied he was making the right decision, he turned his attention to the man on his left.

Hermann Schmidt stood unmoving, chest out, shoulders back, his gaze focused on the far wall. Since serving with Schmidt in the last war, Doenitz had trusted his fellow officer completely. Even at fifty, the man's cold blue eyes, chiseled features and close-cropped blond hair defined Aryan perfection. But it was his unwavering loyalty to the Fatherland that made him an asset to the *Kriegsmarine*.

"These are no longer safe in my office." Doenitz stabbed at the blueprints with his index finger. "Although we don't know exactly what the intruder was after, I am not willing to take any chances."

Schmidt lowered his gaze and considered the drawings in silence. His expression remained neutral throughout his inspection. "Is this the only set of blueprints?"

"No. The engineers who developed the bombs have the originals. For the sake of secrecy, however, only a handful of people have been allowed access to either set."

"Very wise."

"Yes." With silent purpose, Doenitz rolled up the pages, inserted the blueprints into a metal tube and then handed the container to Schmidt. "It is now up to you to keep these safe."

Tucking the cylinder under his left arm, Schmidt nodded. "I will guard them with my life."

"I have no doubt." Satisfied the first part of the meeting was going as planned, Doenitz strode to the map covering the entire south wall of his office. "Germany is at her finest hour, *Kapitän zur See*. It is time the rest of the world experiences the magnificence of our capabilities."

Schmidt smiled with what looked like quiet relish. "Agreed."

"As commander of U-116, you are now among the elite of the *Kriegsmarine*." Dragging his finger along the route Schmidt would take through the English Channel,

Doenitz continued, "You are solely responsible for the success of this secret mission."

"I am humbled by the magnitude of your trust, Herr Admiral."

A perfect answer.

Hands clasped behind his back, Doenitz walked to the row of windows on the north wall overlooking the harbor. Freezing rain scratched a steady rhythm against the glass. The chilling cold slicked ice into twisting patterns, making visibility all but impossible at this early hour. "I cannot stress the importance of keeping the blueprints from falling into the wrong hands."

"I understand."

Returning to the map, Doenitz eyed the coastline bordering the English Channel. Cold fingers of purpose clutched around his heart. "We must wage total war on the enemy."

Schmidt merely inclined his head, waiting patiently for Doenitz to continue. This was the advantage of working with seasoned sailors, men who had experienced the humiliation of defeat. Their devotion to the Third Reich was a given.

"As with your other missions, do not pick up any survivors along the way."

Schmidt gave a quick nod. "I will strive only to take care of my own boat and crew."

"That is all I expect." Hard determination edged his voice up an octave. "Any events during your patrol which are in direct violation of the international agreement should not be entered in your war log."

Schmidt's blue eyes turned cold and impassive. "I will report those to you personally."

"Very good. Now, what is U-116's status?"

"Everything is on schedule. She will be outfitted and ready to sail on the twenty-fourth as planned."

Doenitz clasped the other man's shoulder in a brief show of confidence. "I realize laying mines is not a popular task, my friend. Since the weapon does not cause immediate damage to the enemy, you and your crew may never see the fruits of your labor."

Schmidt threw his shoulders back, exuding an unshakable iron bearing. "I only wish to do my part for Germany, Herr Admiral."

Satisfied at last, Doenitz returned to the cabinet that held the rest of his important blueprints and documents. Before shifting them to their new locations, there was one final matter to discuss with Schmidt.

"Your character and your temperament make you a valuable officer, Hermann," he began carefully. "I am honored to have you among my most trusted men."

"It is an honor to serve under you, sir."

"I understand the sacrifice I am asking of you. But you must dedicate yourself completely to the Fatherland."

Schmidt nodded in understanding. "My personal life will not interfere with my duties."

Ah, the perfect opening. "I trust Elena Kerensky will not be a distraction."

"No, sir." Schmidt looked at him directly, his eyes unblinking. "She understands my duty is to Germany first."

"Good. Good." Deciding to keep his suspicions about

the daughter to himself, at least until he had further evidence to support his theory, Doenitz went fishing instead. "What about her famous daughter? What do you know of her?"

Schmidt's lip curled in disgust. "She is a silly, spoiled girl with very little on her mind."

Perhaps. Perhaps not. Doenitz had his doubts.

"Yet she is at the height of her profession," he pointed out. Reason enough to take her seriously.

"Her beauty has gotten her far," Schmidt conceded. "But like most women of her type, she is easy prey for unscrupulous men. SS men, especially." His ruthless tone said how he felt about the company Katarina Kerensky kept. "She is not overly discreet."

"Is there an SS man in particular that's been sniffing around the actress lately?" Doenitz asked. One who had made the journey to Wilhelmshaven with her recently?

Schmidt's lip curled. "This week or last?"

So Katarina Kerensky ran through men, not unusual considering her profession. "You say she's silly and likes dangerous men, is that all you know about her?" Doenitz asked.

"That's all there is to know. Either she is exactly as she seems or she is a brilliant actress." Schmidt released a snort. "You may decide for yourself, of course, when you meet her tonight. But in my opinion, no one is that good at pretending."

Doenitz would indeed judge for himself. In the meantime, he had other documents to move.

"Thank you, *Kapitän*. That is all for now."

Schmidt tossed out his own arm in salute. "*Heil* Hitler."

Doenitz returned the gesture with equal enthusiasm. "*Heil* Hitler."

As Schmidt left the room at a stiff, clipped pace, Doenitz allowed a slow, cold smile to touch his lips. After tonight he would have his answers about the famous actress. He would find out who she worked for and then he would uncover her reasons for breaking into his private chambers, assuming she was indeed the culprit.

Ah, yes. The trip to Hamburg this evening, the one he'd dreaded a week ago, could very well prove to be an enlightening experience after all.

Rissen, West Hamburg, 0800 hours

In sharp contrast to Katia's mood, the day dawned crisp and bright. She would have much preferred a dark and rainy morning for answering her mother's summons.

A reasonable person would be snuggled in her bed at this hour, or at the very least checking on her wounded partner. Unfortunately, family obligation had been bred into Katia from birth. And as much as she wanted to worry over Friedrich Reiter's meeting with Heinrich Himmler, or wonder how the British spy's wound was healing, she found herself putting off her trip to the *Vier Jahreszeiten* hotel and stepping into the quiet, tasteful foyer of her mother's home instead.

Looking around her, Katia sighed. The decor was as

stylishly equipped as its owner. Lovely and aloof, the pearl-gray marble floor, cream-colored walls and stern-looking antique table suited Princess Elena Dietrich Patrova Kerensky to perfection.

Katia's mother had been given the villa on the Elbe River two years ago, shortly after she'd become a favorite of Adolf Hitler. More showcase than home, the house had everything a Russian princess in exile could want, even if that princess was of German descent with a secret Jewish grandparent in her lineage.

Katia's skin iced over as she stepped farther into the house. Although she had no proof, she imagined this sprawling home had once belonged to a Jewish family taken by the Nazis.

The thought made her sick, made her seem more like an intruder than usual.

How could her mother live with herself? Where was her conscience? Her disgust? Her shame?

Elena's solid position in German society had given her back the life that had been ripped from her during the dark days of the Revolution. She lived in a fairy-tale world again, one similar to that of the Tsars.

Was Elena Kerensky that shallow? Did she not understand the cost others had paid for the opulence she enjoyed now? The same cost she herself would pay if Hermann Schmidt discovered her secret? She had once claimed to be a devout Christian. Her actions said otherwise. Had Elena joined the new German religion, the *Gottglaubig?* Had she become one of the blind millions who worshipped the romantic notions of a pagan past?

Lord, if that's true, what am I to do? How am I to proceed?

Katia's breath turned cold in her body. A scream clawed at the inside of her throat, but she kept her expression bland as she made her way to the front parlor. She could not help but think that her heels clicking against the marble sounded like nails to coffins.

Strict control prevented Katia from reaching up and smoothing the wind-tangled hair off her face. She was an adult now, not some naughty child who deserved scolding. Shoulders back, chin high, she took note of the countless flowers that spilled out of pots and vases on every available tabletop. The colorful blooms presented an impression that the war had not yet touched this part of the world.

How long would Elena Kerensky lie to herself?

Rounding the corner, Katia noted a fire had been laid in the parlor, but was not yet lit. The illusion of warmth came from several lamps shooting beacons of golden light throughout the pristine room. No doubt, the soft ambience was designed to create a soothing, welcoming atmosphere.

Katia had never felt so alone, so empty. So terrified. She didn't think she could continue playing the role of the dutiful daughter much longer. The lie was taking its toll.

Lord, I…I…I pray for courage. As prayers went it was a pitiful attempt. Well, she was feeling rather pitiful at the moment, especially as she watched her perfect, serene mother rise from her chair.

Elena stretched out her hand to beckon Katia forward.

Dressed in a soft tan dress with brown trim, her hair in its trademark upsweep, Elena looked as elegant as always.

"Darling," she greeted. "You are right on time." Her tone was pleasant enough, but her eyes remained distant, guarded even, as they had been the day before.

"I am always on time, Mother."

"So you are."

Katia didn't like how Elena watched her, with her pale eyes looking as though she could see straight inside her mind. Katia had to swallow back a wave of nervousness. Why did she always feel inadequate in the presence of the woman who had given birth to her?

Shaken more than she thought possible, Katia ignored the familiar clutching of her stomach and moved forward to kiss her mother's cheek. "You look well."

"I am well, quite well. And how are you, my dear?"

"The same as always." Petrified. If Elena Kerensky could ignore what was happening around her, then so could every other decent citizen of the Volk.

"Come, Katia, sit. Have some tea." There was no warmth in the invitation.

Unsure what to make of her mother's mood, Katia did as commanded. "As I said on the telephone, I cannot stay long."

"Nonsense." Elena waved off the objection. "Your first obligation is to your family."

Katia gave in, hoping to end this command performance more quickly with compliance. She sat down in a stiff-back chair, but she couldn't stop her hand from fluttering absently over her hair.

Elena's gaze followed the gesture. Pursing her lips in disapproval, she poured tea into a china cup. "You look tired, darling."

Katia curled her toes inside her shoes and clamped her hands together in her lap. "I've had several long nights at the theater."

Elena treated Katia to one of her long silences. Only then did she remember the theater had been dark last night and she'd begged off dinner with complaints of a headache. Would Elena point out the obvious inconsistency in Katia's excuse?

This is what comes of living a life of lies.

Katia held perfectly still and waited. A part of her noticed the servants bustling in and out of the room, making preparations for the party later that evening. The other part of her held her breath in trepidation.

"Yes, darling, I'm sure that must be the reason." Elena placed a cup on a saucer and handed both to Katia. "I don't know why you bother with that ridiculous endeavor. You should be focusing on marriage. You aren't getting any younger."

"I am only twenty-six."

"Long past the age I was when I married your father." A sadness crept into Elena's eyes, but she quickly wiped away the emotion with a determined blink.

Katia fought her own wave of melancholy. She'd thought of her father more in the last two days than she had in the last eighteen years.

"Who would I marry, Mother? Someone like Hermann?" She kept her voice cool and distant, afraid if she allowed her emotions to surface there would be no way to stop them from overflowing into a tangle of words that she could never take back.

Elena's gaze narrowed, but there was no real hardness in her eyes, only a look that Katia couldn't quite decipher. Concern maybe? "You cannot deny that my marrying Hermann will have its advantages," she said at last.

Hands shaking, Katia set her cup and saucer aside. She couldn't hold her tongue any longer. She couldn't. "Would your grandfather agree?"

Calmly, without an ounce of self-consciousness, Elena plucked a linen napkin from the tea service and dabbed at her lips. "Do not be so quick to judge, Katarina. Grandpapa would want me safe. Marriage to Hermann will provide a certain level of protection I cannot achieve otherwise."

Then it was as Katia had suspected. Her mother was hiding in plain sight. With her royal title, Aryan good looks and marriage to a high-ranking Nazi, no one would think to look into Elena Kerensky's past. But what if they did? What if hatred of the Jews increased? What if the Nazi paranoia grew worse?

By marrying Hermann Schmidt, Elena was taking a terrible risk.

A servant dressed in the required uniform of stark black and white swept through the room, moving close to the two of them. Katia waited until she bustled out again.

"Leaving Germany would provide far better protection," she murmured, holding her mother's gaze with unwavering resolve.

Elena blinked. Then blinked again.

Still, Katia held her stare.

For the first time in years, Elena broke their eye contact first.

Katia reached out and squeezed her mother's hand. "It's not impossible."

Elena tugged free. "Don't say such a thing. Don't even think it. The Führer cannot be stopped. Soon, not only Europe but all the world will become a part of the new Germany."

The new Germany? Elena Kerensky's choice of words confounded Katia, especially when there was an unmistakable warning in her eyes. Clearly her mother saw the danger of staying in Germany. Yet she chose to remain.

Why? Did she really believe there was so little hope left? That Hitler could not be stopped, and would take over the entire world?

Katia would never lose that much faith in good overcoming evil. She must trust in the Lord, even when she couldn't hear His voice. No, especially then. Her father's death had been a horrible thing, but he'd died free in his belief. His faith in God had never wavered, not even in the end. God had not abandoned her father, nor had the Lord abandoned her as she'd once thought.

She had been the one to turn away.

Forgive me, Lord.

As much as she wanted to rejoice in her resurrected faith, she had to finish what she'd started here. Perhaps she still could convince her mother to leave Germany. She couldn't live with herself if she didn't try. Driven by a newfound desperation, she went to her mother and placed her mouth next to her ear.

"I can get us out." The words fell from her lips almost without a sound.

"No." Elena drew away, nearly shoving Katia back into her chair.

"Oh, but I could."

Horror filled her mother's eyes and she looked desperately around her, as though there were as many invisible people as the visible servants listening to their conversation. "You speak too boldly."

Her mother was right, of course. The secret police had ways of knowing things they had no business knowing. It would be foolish to let her guard down, even in her own mother's house—*especially* in her mother's house.

Realizing no good would come from continuing the conversation with so many servants meandering about, Katia let the matter drop. For now. "I'm sorry, Mother, I misspoke."

"You are tired, darling." Elena placed her hand over Katia's and squeezed gently. "That is all."

"Yes, that must be it."

Elena nodded. "You should consider marriage," she said again, more vehemently this time. "You could start a family and stop what you are doing, before it is too late."

What an odd choice of words. Either her mother was simply being a concerned mother or Elena Kerensky knew more than she should.

Which was impossible, of course. How could Elena know of Katia's secret life?

"You want me to leave the stage," she asked for clarification. "Is that what this sudden push for marriage is about?"

"Yes." Elena gave a short shake of her head. "I wish for you to quit the stage as well as your other, shall we call them, pursuits?"

Her other pursuits?

Fear congealed in Katia's throat. She was no longer certain of her mother's meaning. She was no longer certain of herself. "Do you…do you know that I…"

She trailed off and took a moment to think.

Her mother couldn't possibly know about her dealings with the British. Katia had been careful. She'd been *more* than careful. And yet the truth was blazing in her mother's eyes, in the silent accusation hanging heavy in the air between them.

"Mother, do you know that I play unusual…roles, on and off the stage?" Katia kept her words vague, in case a nosy servant thought to listen to their conversation.

"Yes, Katarina." Her mother's confirmation snaked between them like the hissing vapor from a steam engine. "I know all about the dangerous *roles* you play," she spoke, lowering her voice to less than a whisper, "for the enemy."

"I…I…I…" She had no words.

Elena dabbed again at her lips with her napkin. "And now that I know, I demand you stop at once."

Chapter Twenty-Two

The cloud of panic that had been hovering over Katia's head for the last two days crashed over her with a force that nearly threw her from her chair.

"But how?" she gasped. "Mother, how do you know?"

When Elena simply stared her, her expression completely unreadable, Katia forgot to play a role. She forgot to breathe. She was a child again, vulnerable and scared and stripped of all her protective barriers. "Mother?"

Elena's expression never changed, but deep lines of worry cradled her mouth. She cut a quick glance at the servant dusting the mantel and then rose abruptly. "Come, darling, I want to show you the decorations I've added to the backyard for this evening's festivities."

Glad to perform such a simple act, Katia followed her mother onto the outdoor deck. She had no idea what to say or do next. It was already too late to be wary. Her mother knew she was a mole for the British. Silence was her only defense now.

Once outside, Elena pulled Katia close, easing her into

the kind of motherly hug she hadn't given her daughter since she was a child.

Katia resisted the urge to cling.

"I have suspected for some time," Elena breathed in her ear. Drawing slowly away, she commanded Katia's stare. "But you confirmed my suspicions yesterday."

Swamped with a fear she'd never known before, not even when the Communists had come for her father, Katia stuttered. "I...I...I did?"

Had she said or done something wrong during lunch, something telling? In so doing had she blown Jack's cover as well as her own?

"It was the roses," Elena whispered.

Katia blinked. The roses. Of course. The hated *white* roses Hermann had given her yesterday morning.

Elena walked to the edge of the deck and placed her hands on the railing. "Your reaction, or rather lack of reaction, was the defining moment for me."

Katia choked in a painful breath of air.

How had this happened? One small mistake, though certainly not her first or even her worst, and now Katia's control of her world was lost forever.

"The roses were your idea," she said softly.

Elena nodded, but she kept her gaze locked on to the horizon. "I couldn't stand living in doubt. I couldn't stand not knowing." She turned to look at Katia, a shadow of an apology filling her eyes. "I had to confirm my suspicions."

Katia could only stand there blinking. The roses had been a trap. Such elemental simplicity.

Katia's throat clenched around a sob. If her own

mother could snare her so easily, surely the Nazis would not be far behind. "Does Hermann know?"

"Of course not. Nor will he ever find out."

A spurt of relief came fast. Nevertheless, Katia chased her gaze around the deck, automatically searching for a hidden enemy that couldn't be found so easily. Paranoia was the legacy of her secret life. Would there ever be a time she wouldn't have to look over her shoulder?

"You play a stupid, dangerous game, Katarina." Elena's voice was no less blistering despite its softness. "Especially with men like Friedrich Reiter courting you at the same time. Unless he, too—"

"He is not a part of what I do." For once, a lie came swiftly and easily off her tongue. A lie that sounded altogether true. Even to her own ears she sounded angry and protective. No, she sounded in love.

Elena gripped Katia's shoulders. "Herr Reiter's pursuit of you is genuine, then?"

Was it? Katia had to think for a minute. He'd gone to Kiel alone, claiming it would be too dangerous for her to go with him. Yet he'd come straight to her when he'd been wounded. He'd revealed his darkest secrets in her bathroom, secrets that could get him killed. And then he'd lowered to his knees and prayed with her.

No intelligent spy would take such risks. And Friedrich Reiter was anything but stupid.

"Yes," she said at last. "His feelings for me are real." *As are mine for him.*

The thought brought her no comfort. Only fear.

But they that wait upon the Lord shall renew their strength...

Elena released a sigh. "Perhaps Herr Reiter is the one you should marry."

What a wonderful, impossible, *terrible* suggestion. If Katia were to marry such a man, she would spend her life in endless worry.

Would that be any different from now?

She hadn't slept last night, knowing he'd gone alone to meet with Heinrich Himmler, knowing his wound could have begun bleeding again and she wouldn't be there to patch him up a second time.

"Perhaps he is the one," she admitted, then quickly shook her head. "It is too soon to tell."

Looking satisfied, Elena pushed her agenda a little harder. "Then you will consider marriage and stop your other...pursuits?"

If only matters were that simple. Katia was already in too deep with the British. She knew too much. They would never let her quit. But it was a truth her mother must never know.

Lifting her shoulder in a careless shrug, she set out to ease Elena's mind. "Yes, Mother, I will consider marriage."

"Good, now let us return to the parlor and finish our tea."

"Mother, wait."

Elena paused.

Katia rushed to her and hugged her close, close enough to whisper in her ear. "Are you a...*Gottglaubig?*"

"To the world, yes. In my heart, no. I am a true Christian." She pulled away and patted Katia on the cheek, a sad smile spread across her lips. "But I will never speak of this again with you."

"I understand." It was enough. It had to be enough.

Yet still, Katia followed her mother into the front parlor with a sense of defeat trailing her. Now that she understood her mother better, fretted for her less, her mind whisked back to another topic. The idea of marriage had been put in her head and she couldn't get it out. She could not marry the British spy, of course. Not as things stood.

He worked for the SS. And although his loyalties might be with the British, he served Heinrich Himmler and Katia could never abide that.

What a complicated, tangled mess. Nevertheless, Katia settled into a benign discussion with her mother about the ball later that evening.

The change in Elena, the obvious relief in her voice, was marvelous to witness. Smiling and nodding, Katia allowed her mother the illusion that she'd convinced her daughter to quit working as a mole for the British. Unfortunately, Katia feared this new trail of lies was as twisted and endless as all the others.

When Elena turned the conversation to the extensive guest list, it seemed to Katia that nearly every high-ranking official in the Third Reich would be in attendance. Her ears pricked as her mother mentioned a familiar name.

"Did you say Admiral Doenitz contacted you personally?" she asked, holding her breath for the answer.

"Yes, he telephoned yesterday. He made a point

to ask me if my famous daughter would be attending tonight."

Caution had Katia speaking very slowly. Her mother already knew too much. "He asked about me," she repeated as she swallowed back the lump in her throat, "directly?"

"Yes. And then he asked to speak with Hermann, something to do with his next command."

Katia knew she should ask about Hermann's orders, not out of politeness but because she might learn something valuable. But as Elena continued chattering, Katia found it impossible to concentrate on the words. Her ears were ringing too loudly.

And then one thought shoved out all the others. Karl Doenitz suspected she'd been the intruder in his room two nights ago. Why else would he make a point to speak with her mother, personally, just to accept an invitation to a party?

Nausea rose in short, sickening waves.

Struggling for composure, Katia stared at the patchwork of light the sun made on the rug at her feet.

What was she going to do?

Get control of herself, that's what. Then she had to find Jack. No, Friedrich. She had to continue thinking of him as Friedrich. Yes, she had to tell *Friedrich* about this new development.

Most of all, she must pray for protection. *Lord, I—*

Elena clicked her tongue, the gesture regaining Katia's attention. "Did you say something, Mother?"

Glancing at the clock on the mantel, she gave a little gasp. "I hadn't realized it was getting so late. I would like to freshen up before Hermann returns from Wilhelmshaven."

"Of course, Mother, I understand."

Elena rose and kissed Katia on the cheek. "We live in dangerous times, Katarina." Her eyes turned fierce and determined. "Remember what I said about marriage."

Katia nodded.

"You know your way out."

"Yes." Katia rose, as well. "I will see you this evening, after my performance."

Elena sighed in resignation. "Very well."

Katia battled against her own emotions as Elena floated out of the room. Too many thoughts collided with one another. Her mother knew she worked for the British. Doenitz knew—no, he suspected—she'd infiltrated his private chambers. Friedrich Reiter knew her secret. And Hermann was due back at any moment.

In less than two days, Katia had lost all control of her life.

Who was she trying to fool? She'd never had control. She'd been deluding herself all along, and had blamed God when things went wrong because of her own pride and arrogance.

Lord, God, forgive me. I have sought security in my own abilities and I have failed. I realize there is no lasting security apart from You.

Almost immediately, she felt the Lord's strength fuse around her, giving her courage.

I cannot do this alone. I pray for Your continued protection and strength.

Feeling less burdened than she had in years, she left the parlor and headed toward the foyer.

Determined to find Friedrich as soon as possible, she picked up her pace. And nearly collided head-on with Hermann Schmidt in the foyer. "Oh."

He steadied her with a firm grip to her arm. "Fräulein. You are in an unusual hurry this morning."

Almost too late she remembered the role she played with this man. "I'm, oh, I'm out of breath." She fluttered her hand in front of her face.

"You should sit." He directed her toward the lone chair in the entryway and then applied hard pressure to her shoulder.

Other than fighting against his touch, she had no choice but to obey. She sat, or rather collapsed, and then looked into the Nazi's gaze.

There seemed nothing unusual in the way he looked at her. In fact, he watched her with the same condescending expression she always saw in his eyes.

"It's rather warm in here." She let out a shaky breath. "Don't you think, Hermann?"

"I hadn't noticed."

Fanning her face with her splayed fingers, she caught sight of the items he'd set by the front door. Her gaze homed in on the metal cylinder propped up against the wall. It was the kind of tube designed to house blueprints.

But what sort of blueprints would Hermann carry at this hour of the day?

"You seem tired, Fräulein. Did you and Herr Reiter have a long evening?"

Oh, he was a clever one, this Nazi. He was testing her. They both knew she'd claimed a headache last night. He thought her stupid. She might as well encourage the misconception.

"Oh, we did." She leaned forward. "In fact, we had a very long night. But don't tell Mother."

"I wouldn't dream of ruining Elena's illusions." His lips pulled into a snarl. "She seems to think you are a good girl."

"Oh, but, Hermann." Katia gave him a sultry look, stopping just short of batting her eyes. "I am a good girl."

He reared back in obvious disgust. "So it would seem."

Playing her role with insipid boldness, she pointed to the metal cylinder. Elena's spoiled daughter would never keep her mouth shut in the face of such a shiny new object. "Oh, look at that, did you bring Mother a gift?"

"No." He yanked the metal tube off the floor with practiced agility. "*This* is none of your business."

"Oh." She hid her interest behind a look of mild curiosity. "Is it something…secret?"

Eyes deadly now, he set the tube out of her reach. "You will not touch this or any of my things. Do you understand?"

"Well!" She drew her bottom lip between her teeth and forced a few tears to the edge of her eyelashes. "You don't have to be rude."

He waved his hand in a dismissive gesture but his

tone turned chilling. "I am not fooled by your little act, Fräulein."

Shock stole her breath. "Whatever are you talking about?"

Try as she might, she wasn't able to hide the tremble in her voice. To add to her distress, her heart quit beating then started again at an accelerated rate.

"We both know you are pretending to be upset, trying to get your way as any spoiled child would do."

She sucked in a relieved burst of air, one that sounded exactly like stunned disbelief. "I don't know what you mean."

"Stop it, Katarina. You are not a child. You are a grown woman who has had her share of male company. Your silly games might work on men like Friedrich Reiter, but they will not work on me."

It would seem the deception she'd woven for the benefit of this Nazi had been more than effective. Continuing the ruse, she blinked up at him in hurt confusion. "You are really quite mean, Hermann."

"Go home, Fräulein." He gave her an impatient glare, the kind men threw at women they had no further use for. "I have important matters on my mind."

He opened the door for her.

"Well, I certainly won't stay where I'm not wanted." Rising, she flicked her hair behind her back and moved past him with her chin positioned at a regal angle.

He banged the door shut behind her.

Katia didn't even flinch. The arrogant Nazi had just made a tactical error in judgment. He thought her ridiculous and harmless, a mistake she would use to her advantage.

She mentally sorted through the pieces of new information she'd just gathered. Fact: Hermann Schmidt was a U-boat captain. Fact: he had been called to Wilhelmshaven for a meeting with Admiral Doenitz himself. Fact: he'd returned with a cylinder designed to carry blueprints.

If the admiral suspected an intrusion in his private chambers, his first order of business would be to shift his most important documents to a safer place. Documents, she surmised, that would include the blueprints of a secret weapon laid by a German U-boat.

Perhaps all was not lost.

Perhaps the Lord had just given Katia the break she needed to complete her mission for the British. If she was able to hold the admiral at bay, she just might be able to pull off the rest.

Oh, please, Lord, let me be right.

Chapter Twenty-Three

Katia didn't find Friedrich Reiter until later that afternoon. By then she was feeling less desperate and filled with conviction. She knew what she had to do. She had to confront the admiral directly.

Would Reiter understand? Or would he try to stop her?

She would find out soon enough.

In order to talk freely, they'd agreed to take a walk together. She knew the picture they made as they strolled along hand in hand. They looked like a couple falling in love. It was not a difficult act for her to play. Friedrich appeared equally ensconced in the role.

Feeling her burdens lift just a little, Katia sat beside him on a bench facing the St. Nikolai Church. She'd like to go inside, kneel before the Lord and offer up her prayers in total subjugation. Except for a few milling tourists, they were virtually alone. But not enough to ignore caution completely.

She settled for drawing strength from the church's magnificent exterior.

Sliding her character into place, Katia turned her head slowly and smiled at her companion with the casual intimacy of longtime friends.

He smiled back, then lifted her hand to his lips.

This is a facade, she reminded herself as a tiny flutter swept through her stomach, *it's not real.*

And yet, she knew she would be devastated when he left Germany. Her heart yearned for all that could never be.

How had this happened? How had she come to the point where she belonged so completely to a man she barely knew?

Cold rays of sunlight had broken through the clouds, but they failed to lighten her mood. Restless now, and more than a little frightened, she shifted on the bench until she looked directly into Reiter's eyes.

He was watching her, his gaze both alert and vibrant. She could almost believe he had not been shot the night before. She knew better, of course. She'd seen the blood flowing down his arm.

Now that the initial shock was over, Katia didn't mind admitting to herself just how scared she'd been when she'd first seen the wound. Thankfully, she'd been able to turn her fear into action. But even now, half a day later, she couldn't let go of the realization that he'd almost been killed.

It was true, then.

She'd fallen in love with the British spy. Stupidly, profoundly, permanently in love. It was the one fight she hadn't prepared for. She had no weapon in her arsenal, no ready-made defense, and certainly no role to wrap around her in protection.

Sighing, she shut her eyes and leaned her head against the bench. She was so tired.

Tired of the games. Tired of the pretenses.

"Last night, you said you trusted me," she began, turning her head just enough to look into his face once again.

He cupped her cheek in his hand. She could see that he was thinking deeply, carefully considering what he would say before he spoke. "I do. I trust you completely."

Oh, how she wanted to enjoy getting to know this man, learning his strengths and weaknesses, what he liked and didn't like. They could grow together in the Lord. But not today. Today, they had serious business looming over them.

"When I was at my mother's this morning, she told me Admiral Doenitz contacted her to personally accept her invitation and to ask if I would be attending the ball tonight."

In a move that spoke of familiarity, he hooked his arm around the back of the bench behind her shoulders and stretched his legs out in front of him. She was not fooled by his outward calm.

He was furious. In fact, the anger vibrating off him was palpable.

"Then he suspects you were the intruder." Aside from anger, there was also worry in his voice. Caring, too.

"I'm sorry," she admitted on a shaky breath. "I went into this mission too arrogant. I should have been more careful from the start."

He was silent for a long time then he squeezed her shoulder gently. "Sometimes setbacks are part of God's plan." His voice sounded thoughtful, as if he was only just coming to his conclusions as he spoke. "Maybe this is the Lord's way of protecting us in a way we cannot fully understand right now."

Rather than shocking her, his suggestion made her want it all. Happiness. Hope. Faith in a sovereign Lord and Savior. She'd lived without God too long, and in many ways she'd done well enough on her own. Until this mission.

In just two days everything had changed.

She still had skills. She still had talent. Her mistake was in thinking she'd ever had control. She knew turning to the Lord for strength was her only answer. But God had let her down so many times.

"I want to, but I don't know if I can trust the Lord completely," she admitted. "How do you stay sure, Friedrich, and confident, especially when you see so much horror all around you?"

There was an uncomfortable moment of silence before he smiled at her. The gesture made his face look so tender, so patient it nearly brought tears to her eyes.

"Make no mistake," he said. "I'm struggling with this, too. In fact, I have spent the last two years angry at God. But I now realize the Lord never abandoned me during those dark days. I abandoned him."

His words were so close to what she'd decided about her own situation. His sincere faith blew past her anger, shoved aside her painful memories and landed straight in her heart. She desperately wanted to believe again.

It was her choice. And she would choose faith.

"Oh, Jack." She gripped his arm, only half-aware she'd used his real name. She would not make that mistake again. Not even in her mind.

"I wish... No." She shook her head vigorously and released her hold on him. Her hope for a future with this man was not a part of the mission. "What I wish isn't important at the moment. Let's get back to our immediate problems," she continued as she shifted on the bench. "What do you suggest we do next?"

For a moment he looked as if he wasn't going to allow her to change the subject, but then he nodded. "First we deal with what we know." He drummed his fingers on her shoulder. "You're absolutely sure you left no physical evidence of your presence in Doenitz's room other than the chair?"

She caught the rhythm of his fingers, tapped her foot along to it. "I've replayed every second I spent in that room over in my mind. I was careful, until the chair."

"Then Doenitz must have made the connection through the guard."

"It's a reasonable conclusion," she said.

Lifting his hand, he brushed his fingers absently down her hair. Stroke. Stroke. Stroke. So soothing. So comforting. She fought to keep her eyes open.

"I want you to stay away from the admiral tonight." However polite he spoke the request, there was an uncompromising glint in his eyes. She knew he would not relent on this.

"But we have to find out whether the admiral truly suspects me," she argued. "Or if his interest in meeting me is merely coincidence. We still have the key to the cabinet. We may be able to go back to Wilhelmshaven for the plans yet tonight." *If they are still there.*

Reiter spoke her thoughts aloud. "It would be a wasted effort. Doenitz will have moved all the important documents after discovering an intrusion. And, Katarina," he spoke, giving her a look of regret. "We have to go on the assumption that he believes he has not only discovered the intrusion but also the identity of the intruder."

Panic crawled over her, sneaking up her spine. "Maybe not. If I could just talk to him I could—"

"You will take no more risks," he said in a clipped, measured tone. "Not on my watch."

His eyes flashed with anger. The sudden, brilliant force of the emotion turned his face into something tough, and potentially mean. This, she decided, was her first real glimpse of the man who worked as Himmler's personal henchman.

She stifled a shiver.

"Then what do you suggest?"

Releasing a slow breath, he regarded the sky with such interest she found herself looking up. When he continued watching the sky she wondered if he was praying.

Before she could ask, he lowered his gaze back to hers. "You will confront the admiral only if I am with you." His eyes turned icy-blue as he spoke. "He will not dare to hurt you with me by your side."

"Just how deep in the SS are you?" She didn't try to keep the fear out of her voice.

She thought she saw something terrible in his eyes,

right before he looked away from her. "I can't tell you that."

She let his words sink in, understood them on an intellectual level, but couldn't prevent the worry from digging deep.

Squeezing her eyes shut, she decided to focus on their conversation and not the danger this man put himself in daily. "There's something else you should know."

He watched her as though he could take her mind apart piece by piece. Fragments of panic swirled up and her fingers twisted in her skirt. It was a telling sign of her nervousness so she stopped.

"Go on," he prompted.

"My mother has discovered my secret life."

He did not react. Nor his body move, not even an inch, but Katia felt the air around him heating. "And Schmidt?" he asked in a low, feral hiss. "Does he know, as well?"

"No." She tangled her hand in her skirt again. This time she couldn't stop the nervous gesture. The gravity of the situation was bearing down on her too hard. "Nor does my mother know about you. She thinks you are merely courting me."

Making a sound deep in his throat, one that was most definitely a growl, he rose from the bench. Without speaking, he tugged her along with him and then steered her toward the harbor.

His gaze locked on the horizon for a long moment. And still he did not speak.

At last, he glanced down at her with genuine pain in

his eyes. He was looking at her with Jack's eyes now. *This* was the man she could adore for a lifetime.

"We have to abort the mission," he said.

"I don't think that's necessary." Although her heart ached, her head worked quickly, weaving facts and possibilities together. "I should have told you this first. Hermann had a meeting with the admiral this morning. When he returned he was carrying a set of blueprints. The metal cylinder was unmarked but my gut tells me that he's carrying the plans to the magnetic mines."

Reiter eyed her with his own unique brand of watchfulness. "You're sure of this?"

"Yes."

"I suppose it's worth checking into." His tone gave nothing away.

Urgency had her switching directions. "I must find out where he put the blueprints."

Jack stopped her with a hand on her arm. "No. It's too dangerous."

"Dangerous?" She gave him a throaty laugh. "The man thinks I'm an idiot. It's his greatest weakness, you know, his inability to see beyond the obvious when it comes to me."

"Katarina, do not underestimate the Nazi. He and the admiral could be setting a trap for you." There was more than anger in his eyes as he spoke. There was fear.

"A trap?" She thought of the way Schmidt had glared at her this morning with obvious disgust. He thought her beyond stupid. "He doesn't have any idea of who I really am. I'd stake my life on it."

"Well, I won't stake your life on it."

"You should have more faith in me."

"Stop and think, Katarina." He gave her one of Jack's looks that grabbed at her heart and twisted. "While you are performing tonight, Schmidt will be at your mother's party. That gives me plenty of time to break into his hotel room and discover if he does indeed have a copy of the blueprints."

Accepting the wisdom of his words, she knew this was no time for ego or foolish arguing. "Hermann is staying at the Hotel Atlantic Kempinski."

Smiling gravely, he threaded his fingers through hers. "If you are right, I could finish this in a matter of hours."

Sadness overwhelmed her at the thought. With the mission complete, this wonderful, courageous man could very well leave Germany tonight. She would never see him again.

Tears filled her eyes.

"Come to England with me," he whispered, pressing a finger to her lips when she started to speak. "No, hear me out. Your mother already knows about your secret life. Admiral Doenitz suspects. It won't be long before others find out. It's no longer safe for you to live in Germany."

His words had her stomach churning with fear. But her convictions were stronger. "I can't leave without my mother. You know this already."

"Take her with you."

"She's determined to marry Hermann."

He pulled in a tight breath. "Then quit. Take no more assignments."

He'd just spoken her mother's greatest wish for her. After these last two days, Katia wasn't sure she didn't wish for the same thing. "They won't let me quit. You know this, also. I am too valuable. And I know too much."

"You could be just as valuable in England. You could train our operatives in German idiosyncrasies. You could teach them the unique body language and other nuances only someone who has lived here would know."

"Why can't you do that?"

His expression closed. "For one, I'm an American. I haven't actually lived in Germany for any length of time. Besides, I have a…different assignment ahead of me."

"What?" Fear edged around her voice. "What is this new assignment?"

"I can't tell you."

"So much for trusting me completely."

"I can't tell you for your protection, not mine." He gripped her shoulders gently and twisted her around to face him again. "I want you safe, Katarina. I *need* you safe."

"No one is safe. We are at war."

Instead of arguing, he stepped back and spread his arms in silent invitation. After only a moment of hesitation, she moved into his embrace and settled her head against his chest.

Folding her close, he kissed the top of her head.

She hugged her arms tighter around him. "You better get moving. There isn't much time now."

"Katarina." He pulled away from her. His eyes were

free of all subterfuge. In fact, he looked vulnerable, like he was about to make a declaration. "Katarina. I—"

"No." She shook her head at him, afraid he would pronounce his love for her, deathly afraid that he wouldn't. "Now isn't the time for speeches. I have to prepare for my performance and you have important photographs to take."

"We aren't finished. Not by half." The soft, affectionate look in his eyes had her gulping for air.

Reaching up, she touched his face.

"If you get the photographs you need," she said, "please don't come back for me tonight. Let this be the end for us."

He took a step away from her, and then another, all the while shaking his head. "I won't let you face Doenitz alone. And I won't leave you behind." His tone brooked no argument on either subject.

In spite of her desire to run away with him, Katia had to think of her mother. "I won't go with you."

"Yes, you will."

"No. I won't." This was one argument Katia had no intention of losing.

Chapter Twenty-Four

After all the mistakes, all the stops and starts, Jack completed his mission for the British in less than three minutes. With the photographs taken and the blueprints returned to the metal cylinder, all he had to do now was exit Schmidt's hotel room undetected.

Pressing his ear against the door, he listened for activity in the hallway. Breathing slowly, very slowly, he counted two sets of footsteps shuffling past. There was a pause, a soft murmur of voices, another pause, subdued laughter, and then the rattle of the elevator doors opening and shutting.

Patting the ridiculously small spy camera nestled safely in his pocket, Jack nudged the door open. With the hallway clear, he retreated in the same manner in which he'd come. Ten purposeful steps and he slipped into the ancient stairwell.

Five minutes later, he walked out the front door of the hotel.

The early-winter air spit at his face. He found the cold

invigorating, as energizing as the adrenaline flowing through his blood.

He crossed at the intersection under the harsh light of a streetlight. He was the picture of a law-abiding citizen with nothing to hide. It was one of his best lies.

Only after he made it to the other side of the street did he stop and allow himself a moment to savor his triumph.

His trip into Schmidt's room had resulted in unprecedented success. Jack not only had photographs of the blueprints to the magnetic mines, but he also had a picture of Schmidt's exact route through the English Channel. The chart containing the carefully plotted minefield, including precise coordinates of where each bomb would be laid, had been hidden with the blueprints.

An unfamiliar wave of doubt rose up. He shoved it back with a growl. With or without the uniform, Jack Anderson was a soldier. His actions would ultimately save thousands of lives.

Lord God, I pray for discernment. Help me to take only the necessary steps to protect the innocent and not to harm them.

That was it. He needed to hold on to God. Daily. What had his father once said? The safest place to stand in a storm was next to the Lord. It was good advice. The only answer in times of war.

Jack allowed a smile to play at the corners of his mouth as he swept his gaze to his right, to his left, and then he glanced at his watch. Three hours to rendezvous.

He stuck his hands in his pockets and started down

the street toward his own hotel. He still had to change into his tuxedo for Elena's party.

Two days ago he wouldn't have hesitated to head straight to the docks and climb aboard a fishing vessel that would take him to meet the British trawler waiting for him in the North Sea.

But that had been before he'd met Katarina Kerensky.

Knowing her had changed him. He had no doubt God's hand had been in their meeting from the start. In the end, Katarina had put a face on the German Resistance for him, and she'd brought a renewed hope to Jack's grim future. He may not survive this terrible war, but he would make sure she did.

Although too many lives depended on what he held in his pocket to risk capture for the sake of a single woman, he couldn't bear to leave her behind, either.

At the very least he could protect her tonight. She would not face Admiral Doenitz alone.

An idea began crystallizing. For once, Jack would use his unsavory connections for his own personal use. And Heinrich Himmler need never know why.

Katia knew her role tonight, and Katarina Kerensky never missed a cue. With a deceptively vacant expression in her eyes, she circled her gaze around the perimeter of the ballroom, taking a quick inventory along the way.

Her mother had outdone herself again. The illusion of happier times was complete, all the way down to the flowers, the elegant music, the glittering crystal and the equally glittering guests.

Thanks to Elena Kerensky's efforts, tonight the hand-picked Germans of wealth, privilege and perfect lineage would find it easy to pretend greatness had returned to the Fatherland.

But not without a price.

Katia's stomach rolled at the thought.

But they that wait upon the Lord shall renew their strength; they shall mount up with wings as eagles; they shall run, and not be weary....

She nodded at her mother's butler, and then waited while he announced her with unnecessary grandeur. The responding hush was a perfect accompaniment for the entrance of a princess turned famous stage actress. One more illusion to add to the others.

Fully in her role now, Katia allowed the guests to admire her long blue gown and upswept hair before stepping forward.

She slowly turned her head, nodding at the faces she recognized. In each cluster of people, she searched for Friedrich Reiter. She came up empty.

Where was he?

Surely he'd been successful tonight. Or had Hermann caught him in the act of breaking into his hotel room?

No. Friedrich was too careful and too good at his job. Katia had no doubt he had succeeded tonight. He would be here soon. But would it be soon enough?

Just as the thought formed she caught sight of Hermann speaking with another naval officer. Even with his back to her, the other man fit Admiral Doenitz's description perfectly.

Her whole body tingled with tension. Beneath the

tension rushed an undertow of doom that built as she glided through the ballroom.

If Friedrich didn't arrive soon she would face the admiral alone. She would do so with the Lord's courage tucked deep inside her.

She repeated her father's favorite verse in her mind. *But they that wait upon the Lord shall renew their strength...*

Even with the Lord's promise nestled within her, she had a sudden urge to turn and run. But then she thought of Jack Anderson and the dangerous role he played as Friedrich Reiter. His sacrifices were far greater than hers. She would not let him down.

As though sensing her eyes on him, the man speaking to Hermann turned to face her. Even at this distance, she could discern the decorations unique to an admiral's uniform. Karl Doenitz. It had to be him. Although shorter than she'd expected, the admiral wore his uniform with terrifying confidence, making him appear far more formidable than Hermann.

Katia continued across the ballroom. Toward the admiral. She found a desperate need to pray. *Oh, Lord, Lord, I need Your courage. I surrender my will to Yours.*

Feeling stronger, she hid the rest of her nerves behind an easy smile. She kept her movements slow and elegant. No one would know her knees were about to buckle under her.

But just as she crossed to the edge of the dance floor, she caught sight of her mother. In spite of a sense of urgency flowing through her, Katia stopped a moment and admired the woman who had given her birth.

How perfect she looked, Katia thought, elegant, refined, with a hint of sadness in her eyes that made her look even more stunning.

A jolt of love came hard and fast, surprising Katia into staring a moment longer. The realization that she wanted to ensure her mother's safety more than her own jumped into her head and convinced her all the more. This was no longer a matter of saving her only surviving parent. This was about saving a woman she loved.

Katia would not allow the war, the Nazis' hatred of Jews, or even Hermann Schmidt to hurt her mother. Even if she died trying, Katia would protect Elena.

Her best option would be to get her out of Germany.

But first, she had to face a suspicious admiral.

It took all her skill as an actress to bury her concerns for her mother and force her mind on the task the lay before her.

Unfortunately, before she could carry on, her mother closed the distance between them and took her hand. "Katia, you look magnificent this evening."

Katia tightened her grip on their linked fingers. "I was thinking the same of you, Mother."

She didn't have the words to tell Elena how much she loved her; too many years had gone by without saying them and too many fresh emotions had been laid bare this morning. Unable to speak, she simply squeezed her mother's hand again.

This time, Elena squeezed back.

They stood still in the moment, mother and daughter connecting on a deeper level than they had in years.

Elena blinked, breaking the spell first, then kissed Katia's cheek. "You are going to be fine, Katarina. Just fine."

"Yes. After tonight everything will change for us both."

They shared a brief, self-conscious hug, then Elena stood back a step and looked around her. "But where is Herr Reiter? I thought he was escorting you this evening."

"An unexpected business matter came up. He will be here shortly." *I hope.*

Katia turned to look around the ballroom. But when she didn't see Friedrich right away her initial confidence turned to worry. He should have completed their mission long before now. "I wonder where he is," she said aloud.

Elena touched her arm. "Not to worry, darling. I'm sure he'll arrive soon enough."

"Yes, he will. He would never let me down." She smiled as she spoke, but she couldn't help wondering what was keeping him. He had seemed so determined to protect her from the admiral.

Please, Lord, please let him be safe.

Short of going in search of him, there wasn't much more she could do at the moment. So she forced her mind to refocus. "Mother, would you mind introducing me to Admiral Doenitz while we wait for Friedrich to arrive?"

"I'd be delighted. He is just over there with Hermann."

Although not especially excited to speak to Elena's fiancé, Katia allowed her mother to maneuver her through the crowd. They were interrupted at least a dozen times, but Elena Kerensky was an expert at charming her guests with a smile and a few words.

All too soon they stopped in front of the admiral. "Herr Admiral," Elena began. "I would like to introduce you to my daughter, Katarina Kerensky."

Doenitz gave her a slight smile, but his eyes remained hard. "Ah, the famous actress. *Kapitän* Schmidt and I were just speaking about you."

Terror threatened to peel the layers of her role away, but Katia forced down the emotion and blinked up at her mother's fiancé. His eyes were sharp on her, weighing and measuring.

Undaunted, she gave him the vacant smile she reserved solely for him. "I trust you said nothing but good things about me, Hermann."

With an ironic twist of his lips, he nodded. "Of course, Katarina. Nothing but good things."

"Well, then, I thank you." She held back from speaking further while her mother continued looking on.

No matter what, Katia would not include Elena in this complicated battle of wills, especially now that her mother knew about her dangerous secret life.

As though sensing Katia's need to speak to the men alone, Elena said, "Well, darling. I'll leave you and Hermann to entertain the admiral while I tend to my other guests."

She gave each of them a brilliant smile before turning to leave. No one but Katia would guess Elena's fear for her daughter. The woman was proving a better actress than Katia herself. She was very proud of her mother.

But now that she was alone with the two Nazis, she felt like a hen trapped in a den full of foxes. Her best weapon was silence.

When both men simply blinked at her, she decided to play shy, as though she was overcome with awe over the admiral.

Ignoring Hermann, she turned her full attention to Doenitz. "I have never met an admiral before." Her words came out soft and a little shaky.

Doenitz lifted his eyebrows. "No?"

"I am quite overwhelmed."

They stared at one another, neither looking away, neither acknowledging Hermann. Katia held on to her smile, adding just the right amount of famous actress to the gesture. She knew this role well.

Doenitz, for his part, continued holding her gaze. To an outsider, they looked enthralled with one another.

Which was true enough, but not for the obvious reasons.

Hermann cleared his throat. "Yes, well, I better help Elena."

Neither Katia nor the admiral responded. Instead, they continued to stare at one another. And stare and stare and stare.

Giving a quick farewell and a promise to return to speak to the admiral before the night was over, Hermann turned on his heel and left.

Once alone, Doenitz broke the silence first. "Your mother is a lovely woman."

Katia was not sure what was in his voice. It was not truth. And certainly not affection. "Yes, she is."

"It would be a shame if anything were to happen to her."

Pretending to misunderstand, Katia steered the conversation toward the mundane. "Are you enjoying the ball, Herr Admiral?"

He clasped his hands behind his back. "I do not wish to sound ungracious, but I much prefer the sea to a crowd of people. And I understand, Fräulein, that you enjoy the sea air, as well." The smile he sent her was as tough and cold as his voice.

Sensing where he was heading, she placed a vacuous look in her eyes. "Why, yes, I do. On occasion."

His smile relaxed only a fraction as he turned to a passing waiter and plucked a flute of champagne off the tray. "I was thinking of a specific patch of sea," he said, handing her the glass. "Along the coast west of here."

She lifted the champagne to her lips, but only pretended to take a sip of the wine. She couldn't afford to be light-headed now that the conversation was steering into unfriendly waters. "Every coastline looks the same to me."

"Ah, but I understand you appreciate our little harbor in Wilhelmshaven more than most."

She lifted a shoulder, even as her breath tightened in her chest. "Perhaps in the summertime."

"I was thinking more in the vicinity of two nights ago."

He knew. The thought echoed in Katia's ears. Round and round, over and over again. *He knew, he knew, he knew.*

Her initial impulse was to inform the admiral she had no idea what he meant, but she decided to stick with the story she and Friedrich Reiter had told the guard that night. "A woman such as myself has to do what she must to find a moment of privacy now and again."

"You don't deny it, then?"

She struggled to keep her tone mild. "Of course not. Why would I?"

"Why, indeed." He spoke evenly, but his gaze turned shrewd and calculating. "If my memory serves, it was very cold that night."

She knew he was leading her down a path, setting a trap. *Be ye therefore wise as serpents, and harmless as doves.* Yes, she would stay one step ahead of this particular snake, by cooperating with him more than he expected. "I think you are correct."

"Perhaps you needed a moment out of the harsh weather?" he said, with just enough menace to send a ripple up her spine.

She twirled the champagne flute in her fingers. "Oh, I had my own ways of staying warm."

Changing tactics, he spun on his heel and offered his arm. "Shall we walk? A bit of exercise is always good for the blood."

Linking her free hand through his, she nodded. "If you like."

They strolled along the edge of the dance floor and then out onto the balcony. She glanced up briefly at the moon. The tiny sliver shone bright against the midnight silk of the sky. Such a lovely evening, she thought, too lovely for the ugly business of war.

"Now that we are completely alone, I will get straight to the point."

She dropped her hand by her side. "I always appreciate honesty."

"There was an intruder in my private quarters two nights ago. I think it was you."

"Me?" She would not panic. "You must be joking."

"I do not joke. And I suggest you don't try my patience. Was it you, or not?"

"Ah," she began, her voice perfectly even, her emotions completely shut down except for one. Anger. She used it to spark indignation in her voice. "What an absurd question."

"Yet, you do not deny you were in Wilhelmshaven two nights ago."

Katia gave a careless shake of her head, lowered her voice to a whisper. "You must understand, Herr Admiral, I was with a special…friend that evening. Which is not something I wish to share with the world. If you capture my meaning."

"So you came to Wilhelmshaven for privacy."

"Precisely."

"Then you won't mind if I check out your story?"

She gave him a carefree shrug of one shoulder. "Do what you must."

"If you would be so kind as to give me your friend's name, we'll end this conversation now. And thereby avoid bringing your mother into this."

For a hideous moment, her mind froze. "My...my mother?"

"I don't suppose you wish for her to be subjected to questioning, now do you? Especially over a simple lover's tryst. And when I say questioning, I'm sure you capture *my* meaning." He left just enough unsaid, hanging in the air between them, to put terror in her heart.

Katia started to give a name, any name, then remembered that the Gestapo already knew the identity of her "lover." It was possible the admiral did, too. "I was with Friedrich Reiter that night."

"And who is this Friedrich Reiter?"

Another burst of panic had the air clogging in her throat.

But then a familiar voice sounded above the pounding of her heart. "*I* am Friedrich Reiter."

Chapter Twenty-Five

Katia whipped around, her gaze landing on the one man she trusted to protect her above all others.

If he'd been successful tonight, he should not be here. He should be on his way to England. But he was here, just as he'd promised. She'd known he would come to protect her, but was he also here to salvage the mission with what little time they had left? Or had he completed their mission? Adding to her confusion, he didn't look like the man she knew. There was something different about him tonight, something almost sinister in his bearing. His eyes had turned hard and ruthless, while his lips curled into a cold, vicious smile that made him look like a, like a...

Nazi.

"And *who* exactly are you?" Doenitz asked.

Forgetting all about the mission, Katia decided she would like to know the answer to that question herself.

"I am SS-*Sturmbannführer* Friedrich Wilhelm Reiter." He gave the Nazi salute. "*Heil* Hitler."

Doenitz returned the salute, and then angled his head. "You claim you are SS, yet you wear no uniform."

Katia's thoughts ran along similar lines, but for very different reasons.

Who was this man, she wondered? She didn't see any of Jack Anderson in him now. What sort of horrors must he endure for this role? How often had he played it?

As if in answer to her unspoken questions, Reiter narrowed his eyes in cold menace. "If you have any doubts as to my identity, Herr Admiral, you may take it up with my direct superior, *Reichsführer* Himmler."

"You work with the *Reichsführer*, directly?"

"Yes."

The hard lines of Doenitz's mouth flattened. "In what capacity?"

Reiter's cold smile disappeared, replaced with a cruel twist of lips. "A little of this, a little of that."

Doenitz's face contorted as if he was in pain. "Am I to assume, then, that you were in Wilhelmshaven with Fräulein Kerensky two nights ago under the *Reichsführer*'s orders?"

Katia held her breath as she waited for the answer along with Doenitz. She knew there was something going on between these two, but she didn't quite understand. And yet, somehow it all made perfect sense. Friedrich Reiter was SS. Karl Doenitz was old-school navy. They would hate each other on principle alone.

For the first time since his arrival, Reiter looked at Katia directly. For an instant, she saw in his eyes the God-fearing man who had begged her to return with him to England, but then the hard SS officer was back in place.

"Perhaps," he said, turning his ruthless gaze back to the admiral, "you should take that up with the *Reichsführer* himself."

Doenitz visibly stiffened. "An excellent idea. If you will excuse me, I have a telephone call to make."

"That won't be necessary, Herr Admiral." Reiter's tone was viciously polite, and in that moment, Katia could very well imagine the man capable of cruelty beyond imagining. "The *Reichsführer* is waiting for you in the ballroom."

On full alert, feet braced for battle, Jack held his position in front of Katarina until Doenitz turned on his heel and left the balcony. Only then did he turn to her. Trying to gauge her mood, he took his time searching her face.

On the surface, she looked breathtaking in the long column of deep blue silk and sparkling diamond jewelry. But on deeper inspection, he noted her narrowed eyes and quick pants for air. She was distressed, more than a little stunned. And very, very frightened. He hadn't expected that last bit. Had Friedrich Reiter scared her? He hated the thought.

"Katarina?"

She muttered under her breath, choked back a sob and then started muttering all over again.

He didn't catch a single word. "You want to try saying that again?"

Pressing her hand to her heart, she took two fast

inhalations and then spoke slower. "He threatened my mother."

Jack knew she was scared. He could feel her fear vibrating between them. But as she fought to maintain her outward calm, he found himself admiring her courage all over again. Katarina Kerensky was an amazing woman. "He won't follow through. Not now."

She spun to glare at him, her eyes wild and just a little unfocused. "He knows it was me. He *knows*."

"He suspects. It is not the same thing." Jack would make sure no harm came to her now, even if that meant taking her back to England with him.

"He'll be back." She all but growled out her response. "And then what will I do?"

"He won't return tonight."

Fire snapped in her eyes. "Why?"

"Himmler and Doenitz have far more serious matters to discuss than a break-in."

Hands shaking, she smoothed the hair off her face. "I… You… You're really SS."

There was no defense against her accusation, other than the truth. "Yes. When in Germany, I answer only to the *Reichsführer.*"

Breathing slower now, she nodded. "I think I understand."

Again, he thought how brave she was—dangerously brave, as was necessary in times such as these.

Needing to comfort her, he reached out.

She shoved his hand away. "I even understand why you couldn't tell me all of it. I just don't like that you're so deeply involved with men like…him."

Jack wanted to defend himself. He wanted to see her look at the man he wanted to be, not the man he was. But there was no reason to argue over something that couldn't be changed. Katarina's ultimate safety depended on getting past this discussion over his identity as an SS officer.

Drawing her deeper into the shadows, he lowered his voice to a whisper. "Just so we're clear, I was successful tonight. Our mission is over."

"I assumed as much." Her tone was filled with relief.

"I leave for England in an hour."

"I understand."

She stepped back into the light, the beacon washing her in its golden glow. With her dignity wrapped around her like a shield, she looked so alone. The reality of her courage tore at him. There was no way he'd be able to walk away from her now. Not without leaving a large part of himself behind. *Lord, fill me with the right words to convince her to leave Germany.*

"Come back with me, Katarina."

Crossing her arms in front of her, she regarded him with blank, patient eyes, giving him the impression that she saw too much of Friedrich Reiter in him now. "I barely know you."

In that she was wrong. Dead wrong. He'd opened his heart to her. Fully. And now he owed her the rest of the truth. His truth. "You know me better than anyone ever has or ever will."

She continued staring at him, her eyes still a little unfocused. But he saw a brief flicker of hope in her gaze, a tiny hint of wavering that gave him the courage to push.

"Come with me," he repeated, pulling her carefully into his arms. "There's still time to make the arrangements. Not much. But enough."

He half expected her to fight him, but she clung to him as tightly as he held her. "You know I can't."

"I'm getting tired of repeating the same argument." Desperation made his voice crack.

"And I'm getting tired of repeating the same answer."

A good military man knew when he'd lost. This battle had been over before it had started. Nevertheless, Jack cared too much to retreat. Even if Katarina ended her work for the British, even if her mother never married Schmidt, Germany was a deadly place for people with Jewish ancestry—no matter how distant.

"You cannot remain much longer." Letting out a breath, he lowered his forehead to hers. "Tonight I've given you a small amount of protection, but it might not be enough over time. They will watch you closer after this."

"Then I lay low for a while." She leaned her head against his shoulder and sighed. "Please. Don't make me explain this to you again. This isn't about you and me. It never was."

"I know."

She laughed, but there was no humor in the sound. "Try to understand. God's will for my life is here in Germany."

Unsure whether to be pleased or suspicious over her

reference to God, he took a deep breath. "This, from you?"

She drew away then fixed him with a direct stare. "You've made a difference in my life, more than you know. I want to believe, I want to have confidence in God again. But I fear it's not enough just to want it."

"Wanting is the first step, Katarina. Come with me. We can find our way back to the Lord together."

"Oh, Friedrich." Her voice softened. "Neither of us have the luxury of putting our needs first."

Jack swallowed. Ached for what he couldn't have. Cleared his throat. Then forced a smile. "I can't change your mind, can I?"

"No."

He was going to fail. No, he *had* failed. He knew that now. Accepted it at last. But he also knew he would return to Germany in less than a month, fully ensconced in his alter ego. He would find a way back to her. The thought made their parting easier. "I'll pray for you. Every day."

"I… Thank you. And I'll do the same for you." She came to him again, wrapped her arms around his waist. "It's not our time."

Cloaked in the shadows again, he pressed his lips against her temple. "There will be a day when this war is over. And then—"

"It will be our time to be together."

"Yes." He held her for a moment longer, just held her as a twisted, frightening mixture of hope and loss tangled together in his heart.

He didn't want to leave her.

He didn't have the right to take her with him. Like she said, this wasn't about them.

God had given each of them a calling for their lives, at a time that required them both to think beyond themselves. They'd been blessed to have these three days.

Shifting her weight, she leaned back to look into his eyes again. "You should probably take your leave at this point."

Yes, he would go. But not before he made it perfectly clear that he was her future. And she was his. He lowered his head and kissed her fiercely on the mouth. Gathering control, he set her at arm's length, but kept his hands on her waist. "This isn't the end for us. I won't say goodbye."

"Neither will I." She touched his lips and then kissed him where her fingertip had been. She kissed him again, tenderly, softly, so softly he trembled.

Silent promises passed between them. Jack believed the Lord would bring him back to her. Someday. The thought gave him the necessary strength to turn and leave her behind.

Chapter Twenty-Six

Jack made it halfway through the ballroom before he was stopped by a soft, feminine voice coming from behind him. "Herr Reiter, I would like a word with you before you leave."

He turned, very slowly, and came face-to-face with Elena Kerensky. He could say many things to this woman, demand even more; instead he kept silent and studied her in candid appraisal.

Tonight she wore her hair pinned in some fancy style of the day. She was dressed in a sparkling silver dress adorned with jewels the color of her eyes. All that was missing to complete the picture of a royal princess was the tiara.

But as regal as the woman looked on the surface, her wide blue eyes blinked up at him in… Jack couldn't put a word to the expression. Fear, perhaps? No, something far more complicated than that.

"I am at your disposal, Princess." He gave her a short bow. "What is it you wish to discuss?"

"Not here," she said. "Follow me."

"Of course."

As she led him out of the ballroom, Jack looked around him. He wasn't usually sentimental, or poetic, but Elena Kerensky had created an old-world charm that caught his imagination. It was as though he'd been transported back in time.

The air shimmered with the golden light of hundreds of candlesticks. Small tables had been arranged in sets of three, the groupings then separated by an assortment of ornamental trees. Flowers of various colors had been strategically placed throughout the room. While a full orchestra played classical music, mostly Austrian waltzes.

The irony was not lost on him. He found himself smiling cynically as she led him to a small alcove just off the front entrance. The spot was not entirely private, but private enough, as long as they kept their voices down.

For a moment she simply gazed into his eyes. He let her.

"You and I, we are alike, I think," she said at last.

Now that was an interesting comment, one that sent the hairs on the back of his neck bristling. "How so?"

"We do what must be done in these difficult times." Her words were strong enough, but her tone lacked edge. "We align ourselves with whom we must."

In that moment, Jack realized Elena Kerensky was not the hard woman he'd once thought. She was simply trying to protect her daughter. His respect for her traveled up a few notches.

"The world is not always as black and white as some would have us believe," he said in response.

"No." She nodded. "It would seem we are of a similar mind."

"Not so much of a shock when one considers our common interest in Katarina."

"No. Not a shock at all." Elena smiled, just a little. A very little. "You realize, of course, I am not completely blind in my daughter's feelings for you."

His protective instinct reared, but he shoved it behind an easy smile. "Katarina is a brave woman. I admire her greatly."

"Admire her?" Parental outrage hummed between them. "That is all you feel for Katarina, mere admiration?"

"No. That is not all. Far from it." He did not elaborate, but he allowed his feelings to show in his eyes. He would not lie about something so important as his love for Katarina. It was the one truth he could have whether he was Jack Anderson or Friedrich Reiter.

"You are a very careful man, Herr Reiter." She nodded in approval. "It is a fine quality to have in these troubling times."

"It has served me well."

"I find it necessary to ask you to be a little less careful."

He waited for the rest.

"Are your feelings strong enough for my daughter to encourage you to do whatever it takes to ensure her safety?"

The desperation in her eyes was at odds with her smooth tone. Clearly, Elena Kerensky was trying to say something more here, something important, but Jack didn't have the time or the inclination to sort through the subtext of her words. "Princess Elena, I am not your enemy. Please, say what you need to say."

She gave him one small nod. "I could not help but notice that you arrived tonight with the *Reichsführer*. Am I to assume you are an officer in the SS, in spite of your lack of uniform?"

Jack inclined his head, wondering why Schmidt had not shared that information with her himself. "You would be correct in your assumption."

"I see." Obvious relief filled her gaze. Jack had not expected that. The woman was proving a surprise, much like her daughter. They were an amazing pair.

"Then perhaps…" Elena trailed off in order to take a deep breath. "*Perhaps* you will take the final step to ensure Katarina's safety?"

Did she know of her daughter's work with the British? Or was she simply taking an obvious step by aligning her daughter's future with that of an SS officer?

Every cell in his body stood at attention. "What did you have in mind?" Although he sensed her response before she spoke again.

"Will you marry her, Herr Reiter?"

And there it was. The solution to all their problems. So simple. So obvious. Of course it would come from Elena, a woman securing her own future in the same way she'd just suggested for her daughter.

Jack allowed the idea to settle in his mind. *Is this it, Lord? Is this the answer I've been praying for?*

If Katarina would not leave Germany, marriage to a

high-ranking Nazi—say, a major in the SS—would give
her a level of protection she would not have otherwise.

With Jack's direct ties to Heinrich Himmler, no one
would look into her background, or her mother's. Even
if they tried they would never get past Jack, or rather,
they would never get past SS-*Sturmbannführer* Friedrich
Wilhelm Reiter.

"Yes, Princess Elena, when I return to Hamburg I will
do everything in my power to marry your daughter."

It was the easiest promise he'd ever made. Unfortunately, he had no idea when he would be able to follow
through.

*23 November 1939, 0830 hours, The English Channel,
three miles off the coast of Harwich*

The wind blew in from the north, howling viciously
and punching Jack in the face. Amid the eight-foot swells
and overcast sky, the low, steady thunder of *HMS Bas-
set*'s engine was underscored by the angry pounding of
water against the hull.

Facing into the wind, Jack took a deep breath. The
heavy scent of diesel fuel overwhelmed the salty smell
of the sea air and did nothing to settle his mind.

Where was the relief? Where was the pleasure over
a successful mission completed?

Back in Hamburg with Katarina Kerensky, that's
where.

He wanted to return to her. He wanted to be with her,
always. But he had to be patient. He had to trust the Lord
would, indeed, guide Jack back to her.

Unfortunately, there were no guarantees in war.

Lord, he prayed, *protect Katarina in my absence. We've both come a long way in our faith, but we still have far to go. Soften each of our hearts to You so we may know Your love, regardless of these dark times in which we live. Give us strength to make the sacrifices we must make for You and Your people. Thy will be done.*

"We're nearly there, Lieutenant."

Jack whipped around. He'd been so caught up in praying he hadn't heard the captain come up behind him. Unforgivable. No matter how deep his personal anguish, he should have been more alert. A mistake like that in enemy territory could get him killed.

"Would you care to join me at the helm for the completion of our journey?"

Welcoming the distraction, he nodded. "Of course."

Twenty minutes later, Jack jumped out of the trawler and onto the military dock near Harwich, only to find the head of MI6, Stewart Menzies himself, waiting for him on the quay.

Struck by the anxious look on the director's face, Jack's thoughts leaped immediately to Katarina and he closed the distance between them in a split second. "Did something go wrong after I left Germany?"

"I'll explain in the car," Menzies said, turning away before Jack could question him further.

For the first time in years, Jack felt real terror.

And there was nothing he could do to alleviate his fears but wait for the British spymaster to give him more information.

Jack had never felt so powerless. But as Menzies took

his time settling into the back of the Bentley, Jack's temper began to burn away his panic. He buried the impulse to strangle the information out of the other man and waited for the Brit to make the next move.

Once the car was in motion, Menzies finally acknowledged him. "You have the photographs with you?"

Straight and to the point. In spite of his frustration, Jack appreciated the frank approach. "Yes. I was also able to obtain the exact coordinates of the minefield that will be laid in the next few days along the Thames Estuary."

"Then the mission was a success."

There was something in Menzies's eyes that put Jack instantly on alert. Looking out the window, he noted that they were traveling directly parallel to the coast, rather than west toward London. "Where are you taking me?"

Menzies leaned back in his seat and gave a careless shrug. "Let's just say I have a surprise for you."

Jack's eyes cut from Menzies to the passing scenery then back to Menzies again. "I beg your pardon, sir, but I've had enough surprises in the past three days to last a lifetime."

"Rest easy, Lieutenant. We are headed to Shoeburyness, where one of the magnetic mines was found imbedded in the mud along the shore."

Jack relaxed his shoulders. "How much of the device is left?"

"It's completely intact."

A wave of disbelief crested, but then gave way to anticipation. What were the odds of finding a magnetic mine in full working condition? A thousand to one? A million to one?

It was incredible.

No. It was a miracle. God had provided the British with a miracle.

Thank You, Lord.

"We have your entire team already in place," Menzies continued. "Lieutenant Commander Ouvry of the Royal Navy has volunteered to diffuse the bomb for us. And if he fails—"

"I'll step in."

Menzies gave him a sly smile. "I thought you might say that. But for Ouvry's sake, let us hope it doesn't come to that."

Jack sent up a prayer for Ouvry's protection, then fell into silence. The mission had come full circle. Just four days ago Jack had stood on the shores of the Isle of Wight surveying the remains of an American cargo ship, one of over a hundred civilian vessels blown up in the last three months.

Now all Jack had to do to prevent further losses was to finalize his countermeasures. And once he did, the *Kriegsmarine's* deadly secret weapon would be rendered useless.

God's will be done!

15 December 1939, war room, Whitehall, London 1400 hours

"I understand your countermeasures are operational."

"Yes, sir." Jack studied the man on the other side of the desk. Although he'd met with him on several "unofficial" occasions through the years, this was Jack's first official meeting with Winston Churchill.

Churchill lit his cigar then took several short puffs. The resolute expression on his face fit his craggy features to perfection. "Let us pray this will buy us the time we need to stop Hitler's attempt to cut off our islands from the rest of the world."

"If I can speak frankly, sir, Hitler has underestimated the British."

"True enough." Churchill's expression turned intense as he opened the file on his desk. "I see you gave us a detailed and accurate report of the minefield laid by U-116 last month."

Jack nodded. Hermann Schmidt's efforts had been wasted. Jack couldn't think of a more fitting end to the magnetic mine mission.

"And because of that information," Churchill continued as he tapped the top page of the report, "we have successfully rerouted dozens of supply ships in the last two weeks."

"I didn't do it alone," Jack quickly pointed out. "Without Katarina Kerensky's help, the mission would have failed."

"I see she made quite an impression on you."

"Yes." And he desperately wanted to return to her. Three weeks had passed since he'd seen her last. It felt like a lifetime.

Closing the file, Churchill leaned back in his chair. "I have been informed that your next mission is set."

"I leave for Berlin in two days." And as soon as humanly possible he would find Katarina.

Churchill rose. "Be very sure this is what you want to do, Lieutenant." He came around the desk and settled his hand on Jack's shoulder. "Once you're inside the SD, you will be on your own. Jack Anderson will cease to exist."

Jack kept his gaze steady. "I understand." It was the price he'd expected to pay the day he'd become Friedrich Reiter. This was the mission MI6 had trained him for these last two years. There was no turning back now.

"Send what information you can, but your main objective will be to sabotage from within."

Jack nodded. It was a dangerous mission, one that could end in his death.

Never will I leave you; never will I forsake you.

He would not go into Germany alone.

Churchill spoke his thoughts aloud. "Well, then, Lieutenant, may God go with you."

Jack rose and gladly shook hands with a man some called a warmonger but who Jack considered one of the bravest, most steadfast men he had ever met. "I pray we see one another on the other side of this war."

"For both our sakes, I hope it is soon, Lieutenant." Churchill's eyes darkened with worry. "I hope it is very soon."

Chapter Twenty-Seven

16 February 1940, Berlin Theater, Berlin, Germany

For Katia, every night was the same. Perform her role. Take her bows. Greet her fans backstage.

Night after night, the audience came to watch her become a tragic heroine of a masterfully written play. Night after night, she gave them what they wanted.

While taking her bows, she squinted past the floodlights into the audience, looking for the one man she couldn't seem to forget.

She feared he wouldn't be there. But no matter how many days passed, no matter what city she was in, Katia never gave up hope of seeing Friedrich Reiter again.

He was in her mind always, even as she continued her clandestine work for the British. Over the past months, she'd completed four more missions for MI6. She had worked alone each time. Thanks to her part in the success of the magnetic mines mission, the British trusted her again. And thanks to Friedrich's efforts at her mother's ball in November, Admiral Doenitz had given Katia no more troubles.

Small compensation for a broken heart.

At least her relationship with her mother was healed. Although against the union from the start, Katia had stood as Elena's witness at her wedding to Hermann Schmidt. That day, Katia's heart had broken a little more. She only prayed marriage to Hermann would be enough to protect Elena from the death camps.

No. She would not give in to depressing thoughts now. Elena had made her choices and Katia had made hers. Their individual futures were in God's hands now, the safest place to be in these dark times.

If only Katia could meet Friedrich again and see for herself that he was safe. Oh, how she missed him, how she feared for him. How she wished there was no war separating them.

Lord, is he safe? Please, I pray You keep him safe throughout the duration of the war and beyond.

As she joined the rest of the cast backstage, Katia skimmed her gaze across the milling crowd. Elegant women wearing their jewels and furs clung to men dressed in tuxedos and various military uniforms. *Luftwaffe. Waffen. Gestapo.*

SS.

Tonight, Heinrich Himmler himself was among the crowd. He was wearing the black uniform of the Gestapo. Small of stature, unassuming, it was hard to believe he was the architect of Germany's greatest horrors.

Out of habit, she tried to determine the identity of the other Gestapo officer with Himmler, but the man had his back to her. The hard jolt to her heart made her breath catch in her throat. Could it be him?

She tried to think logically, but the pounding in her head made it difficult. There was something painfully familiar about the tall, broad-shouldered officer. And yet, she couldn't allow herself to hope. She'd been through this routine countless times in the last three months.

Too many nights she'd thought she'd seen Friedrich Reiter. Too many nights she'd been wrong. And left with only a prayer for his continued safety.

But, this time, as the man turned slowly around, her whole body relaxed on a sigh.

He'd come back to her.

He took a single step toward her, one step was all, and the shadows fell away from his face. His sharp, serious eyes and tall, lean body reminded her of a big, beautiful cat.

Code name, Cougar.

She remembered it all now. The tension-filled first meeting, the various battles for control, the ultimate agreement to work as a team, the trip to Wilhelmshaven, praying together on her bathroom floor. And, of course, the promise that he would return to her someday.

She didn't particularly like how comfortable he looked in the Gestapo uniform. Nor did she like the fast jolt of fear that pressed against her chest.

What was he thinking, becoming a member of the SD? If caught, he would be tortured, and eventually killed.

The noble fool.

As he began pacing toward her—slowly, deliberately—her heart stopped beating. Then he halted in front of her and she thought her heart just might beat right out of her chest.

"Katarina, you look as lovely as I remember." The words rolled off his tongue in perfect German, the hint of Austria clinging to the edges just as she remembered.

She swallowed back her nerves. "Welcome to Berlin, Herr Reiter."

He took her left hand in his, kissed her knuckles and then looked at her with Jack Anderson's eyes. "I've missed you, my darling."

Said so simply, she had no doubt he meant every word. For propriety's sake, she knew she should take her hand back. But she badly needed to absorb the contact. "I've missed you more."

He chuckled at her response. "Always so competitive. It's what I love most about you."

Massaging her bare ring finger with his thumb, his face broke into a smile. "I think it is long past time I purchased you a piece of jewelry."

She put her heart in her eyes and reached up to cup his cheek. "I wouldn't refuse anything from you."

Still smiling, he pulled her hand away from his face and placed it against his chest. "I can't live without you, Katarina. I've tried. I've failed."

He did not look like a beaten man. In fact, he looked rather pleased with himself.

"Well, then, perhaps you should quit trying and admit your defeat once and for all," she said.

"My thoughts precisely."

The tenderness in his eyes made his intentions all too

clear. Katia's throat swelled. But then she was bumped from behind. Realizing how many people could be watching them, she sighed in frustration. "I think we should finish this conversation in private."

"Your ability to read my mind is quite impressive."

"It's not really so amazing." She gave him the gentle smile of a woman in love. "We merely think alike, Herr Reiter."

"So it would seem," he said, lifting a single eyebrow. "Now, about that privacy you suggested?"

Smiling, she took his hand in hers and led him to her dressing room.

He shut the door behind them with a firm click.

With her heart racing from anticipation, she turned to face him. Leaning slightly forward, her body seemed to have a mind of its own, as though it was answering the powerful pull of her soul mate.

And then…and then…

He tugged her into his arms.

Just like that, her world felt a little less dark. She pressed her cheek against his chest. "Welcome back, my darling."

He pulled away and then kissed her firmly on the mouth. "I love you," he said in a strong voice. "I should have said it before I left you the last time."

She looked into his eyes and saw the godly man that had helped her believe again. "I love you, too." How could she not?

"Marry me, Katarina."

She didn't want to refuse. But she was afraid of the uncertainty that lay ahead of them. "What about your…

journeys?" She spoke carefully, taking great pains not to mention England in case the Gestapo was listening to their conversation. "To distant places."

"My traveling days are over. I am to stay in Berlin for the duration of the war." He gave her a grave look, one that left little doubt to the underlying meaning of his words.

Recognizing the danger he was putting himself in, she fought back a wave of panic.

"Don't look at me like that," he begged. "I have every intention of growing old with you."

She nodded, and found she needed to draw in a long breath before she had the ability to speak again. "Growing old together is a lovely ambition."

"Katarina, take a chance on me. Take a chance on us. It would certainly make your mother happy." One corner of his mouth kicked up in an ironic grin.

So her mother *had* talked to him before he'd left Hamburg. Katia did not blame Elena for trying to protect her daughter in the way she thought best.

Even if Katia wasn't in love with the man, the idea of marriage to an SS *Sturmbannführer* would still make sense. To the Nazis, their union would look like the coveted blending of an Aryan elite with Russian royalty. To Katia's mother, their marriage would be an added layer of protection from the concentration camps.

To Katia, marrying Friedrich Reiter would be all about love. "Yes. *Yes*. I will marry you."

For a moment he only watched her, his gaze alight with pleasure. "I pray I prove worthy of you, Princess Katarina."

She thought of the courage he'd displayed on countless occasions. She thought of the way he'd knelt at her feet in her bathroom and taught her how to pray again. "You have already done that, my love. But now I have one small request of you."

He raised her hand to his lips. "Anything."

"Stay alive."

His gaze filled with the conviction of Jack Anderson. "God led us to one another, Katarina." He kept his voice barely above a whisper as he spoke. "We must believe He will lead us through this war, as well."

She loved his confidence in the Lord. It gave her the courage to hope.

As though God Himself reached down and wiped away the last of her fears, Katia felt certainty spread through her. She wouldn't think about the end of the war or all they stood to lose. She would take each day as it came and would fit a lifetime into every moment she had with this man. "Let's get married as soon as possible."

He enfolded her in the shelter of his warm embrace and spoke softly in her ear. Even if someone listened, they wouldn't be able to discern his words. "Our battles are only beginning, but we will never fight them alone. We have each other and we have the Lord."

"Now that's something worth putting our hope in."

* * * * *

Dear Reader,

Thank you for taking the trip to Nazi Germany with me. I hope you found inspiration in Katia and Jack's story. I truly believe they are two of my most heroic characters to date. I hated to leave them in the midst of the war, but I promise you they survived Hitler and his Nazi war machine. In fact, they moved to America in December 1945 and settled in southern California. Katia's mother, a war widow by early 1944, made the journey with her daughter and son-in-law. She lived to the ripe old age of ninety-three, but never looked a day over sixty.

Tired of death, Jack studied to become a heart surgeon. He saved hundreds of lives during his long career. Katia went on to be a successful film star. She retired at the age of thirty-two so she could focus on her family. The Andersons produced five children and eighteen grand-children, three of whom are in the military today.

So you see, our hero and heroine might not have met under the most romantic conditions, but their love carried them through a brutal war. They lived a long and happy life together.

Although fictional, Katia and Jack represent all the brave men and women of the German Resistance who didn't look the other way or fall in line when Hitler took over their country. Praise God for their courage.

I love hearing from readers. The easiest (and quickest) way to contact me is at www.ReneeRyan.com.

All the best,
Renee

QUESTIONS FOR DISCUSSION

1. Why do you think Katia doesn't trust Jack at their first meeting? Is it something he does, in particular, that makes her skeptical, or is it her situation in general? What has brought these two together? What is at stake if their mission fails?

2. What secret is Katia harboring? Considering the setting and time period, what sort of risks does her secret bring? What does she have to lose if her secret is revealed?

3. What sacrifices has Jack made to become a spy for the British? Do you think his crisis of faith is legitimate? Why or why not? What would you do if you found yourself in a similar situation?

4. What has driven Katia to rely on herself rather than God? How does she compare Communist Russia to Nazi Germany? What scares her most about the Third Reich?

5. Where do Jack's true loyalties lie? What has driven him to lose his way? Why does he struggle with the question of whether he's a traitor or a hero?

6. What problem does Katia's mother pose for her undercover work? What added glitch does her recent engagement present? Why does the timing of this

announcement make Katia suspect her own mother is in league with the Nazis?

7. What are the similarities between an actress and a spy? What are the differences? Do you think Katia's training as a stage actress benefits her? She claims she's played so many roles she doesn't know who the real Katia is below the actress. Do you think this is true? Why or why not?

8. What parallels do you see between Jack and Hermann Schmidt? Where would you draw the line between serving God and country versus allowing country to become God? Do you think the latter is what happened in Nazi Germany? Why or why not?

9. Are the rules different for Christians in times of war as opposed to times of peace? Is there ever a situation where lying is acceptable? Why or why not?

10. When Jack and Katia suffer several failed attempts at getting a photograph of the plans for the Nazi secret weapon, Jack decides to finish the job on his own. Do you think that was a valid decision on his part? Were you surprised Katia was the one to discover the alternate location of the plans? What complications did this discovery pose for Jack?

11. Did you sympathize with Katia's reasons for turning down Jack's offer to leave Germany with him? Why or why not?

12. Katia and Jack get their happy ending, however, the war is just heating up. What challenges do you see ahead of them?

Love Inspired.
HISTORICAL

TITLES AVAILABLE NEXT MONTH
Available October 12, 2010

PRAIRIE COURTSHIP
Dorothy Clark

WYOMING LAWMAN
Victoria Bylin

REQUEST YOUR FREE BOOKS!

2 FREE INSPIRATIONAL NOVELS
PLUS 2
FREE
MYSTERY GIFTS

Love Inspired HISTORICAL

INSPIRATIONAL HISTORICAL ROMANCE

YES! Please send me 2 FREE Love Inspired® Historical novels and my 2 FREE mystery gifts (gifts are worth about $10). After receiving them, if I don't wish to receive any more books, I can return the shipping statement marked "cancel". If I don't cancel, I will receive 4 brand-new novels every other month and be billed just $4.24 per book in the U.S. or $4.74 per book in Canada. That's a saving of over 20% off the cover price. It's quite a bargain! Shipping and handling is just 50¢ per book.* I understand that accepting the 2 free books and gifts places me under no obligation to buy anything. I can always return a shipment and cancel at any time. Even if I never buy another book, the two free books and gifts are mine to keep forever.

102/302 IDN E7QD

Name   (PLEASE PRINT)

Address   Apt. #

City   State/Prov.   Zip/Postal Code

Signature (if under 18, a parent or guardian must sign)

Mail to Steeple Hill Reader Service:
IN U.S.A.: P.O. Box 1867, Buffalo, NY 14240-1867
IN CANADA: P.O. Box 609, Fort Erie, Ontario L2A 5X3
Not valid for current subscribers to Love Inspired Historical books.

Want to try two free books from another series?
Call 1-800-873-8635 or visit www.morefreebooks.com.

* Terms and prices subject to change without notice. Prices do not include applicable taxes. Sales tax applicable in N.Y. Canadian residents will be charged applicable provincial taxes and GST. Offer not valid in Quebec. This offer is limited to one order per household. All orders subject to approval. Credit or debit balances in a customer's account(s) may be offset by any other outstanding balance owed by or to the customer. Please allow 4 to 6 weeks for delivery. Offer available while quantities last.

Your Privacy: Steeple Hill Books is committed to protecting your privacy. Our Privacy Policy is available online at www.SteepleHill.com or upon request from the Reader Service. From time to time we make our lists of customers available to reputable third parties who may have a product or service of interest to you. If you would prefer we not share your name and address, please check here. ☐

Help us get it right—We strive for accurate, respectful and relevant communications. To clarify or modify your communication preferences, visit us at www.ReaderService.com/consumerschoice.

LIH10R